The Adventurous Deeds of Deadwood Jones

The Adventurous Deeds of

DEADWOOD JONES

Helen Hemphill

FRONT STREET
Asheville, North Carolina

Also by Helen Hemphill

Runaround

Long Gone Daddy

Printed in the United States of America
Designed by Helen Robinson
First edition

Library of Congress Cataloging-in-Publication Data

Hemphill, Helen.
The adventurous deeds of Deadwood Jones / by Helen Hemphill. — 1st ed.
p. cm.
Summary: Thirteen-year-old Prometheus Jones and his eleven-year-old cousin Omer flee Tennessee and join a cattle drive that will eventually take them to Texas, where Prometheus hopes his father lives, and they find adventure and face challenges as African Americans in a land still recovering from the Civil War.
ISBN 978-1-59078-637-6 (hardcover : alk. paper)
[1. Cowboys—Fiction. 2. Cattle drives—Fiction. 3. African Americans—Fiction. 4. Race relations—Fiction. 5. Cousins—Fiction. 6. Wheeler, Edward L. (Edward Lytton), 1854 or 5–1885—Fiction. 7. West (U.S.)—History—1860–1890—Fiction.] I. Title.
PZ7.H3774487Adv 2008
[Fic]—dc22
2008005422

FRONT STREET
An Imprint of Boyds Mills Press, Inc.
815 Church Street
Honesdale, Pennsylvania 18431

For Neil

CONTENTS

The Adventurous Deeds of Deadwood Jones

CHAPTER ONE

Some devilment sends me packing.

"Halleloo!" Omer grins, wide and proud. "That sure is some fine riding, Prometheus!" A string of sweat shines down one side of his forehead into brown eyes the color of oiled leather.

I throw my leg over the filly's back and slip to the ground while Omer slides a rope over Miss Stoney's neck and hands her off to Pernie Boyd Dill.

"Got my four bits?" I ask.

"I ain't paying four bits for you to break a filly." Pernie Boyd sets his wide-brimmed hat on the back of his sandy hair and rests his hands on his hips. He bears the same ferret-eyed stare and pitted skin as his daddy. "You getting dreadful sassy, Prometheus Jones." Pernie Boyd talks big, as long as his brother, LaRue, is nearby.

LaRue spits tobacco into the dirt. "You're getting nothing," he says. LaRue is as comely as his brother is ugly, with yellow curly hair, pale water-gray eyes, and a heart-shaped mouth. He parades around like a pretty boy with a ruffled shirt and shiny pat shoes.

I call up an evil spirit and wish it on LaRue. Omer unfastens the loop of a new snake whip from his belt and runs his hand over the belly and down the fall. He don't look up. Omer don't like the Dill boys much—not since they poisoned off his best hunting dog.

Pernie Boyd steps into his brother's shadow. He's scared of Omer and me, even though he's a full year older than either of us. He's scared of all Negroes. "You better not lay a hand on me!"

"We ain't paying you any money," LaRue says. "Didn't you hear me, slave boy?"

I ain't their slave boy. I ain't never been their slave boy. I was born on the day Mr. Lincoln made his Proclamation, and I've been free since my first breath. Mr. Lincoln done won that war, and Colonel Dill done lost half his land and most all his gold money. But that don't matter to me. The Dill boys still owe me four bits.

"He speaking for you?" I say over to Pernie Boyd.

Pernie Boyd looks up at me, uncertain. "Figured Miss Stoney would break your neck. I ain't got no silver," he says, stuffing his hands deep in his britches to hide his lying. "All I got is my lucky rabbit's foot, and I won't part with that."

But Pernie Boyd stares at Omer's rawhide sure enough and starts flapping his pockets, airing out his jitters. Pernie Boyd pulls the rabbit's foot out of his pocket and holds it up for Omer to see. "It's a good rabbit's foot, too. Cut off the left hind leg during a full moon. Old man sold it to me said it's full of hoodoo magic. I'm safe as a baby." LaRue's worrying with Miss Stoney's bridle and don't look up. Pernie Boyd hides the rabbit's foot in his hand, then sneaks it back in his pocket. "Ain't nothing but good come looking for me."

He glances over at LaRue, then at the whip, then at me, then at the whip again and bites back his lip. Pernie Boyd was born yellow-dog fearful.

"I know!" His words come out all at once. "I got a jim-dandy idea! I got a raffle ticket you can have. Come from old man Levi. He's offering a fine horse worth thirty dollars. It's a beaut—black stallion with two strong hindquarters. Ticket's not even cold; I bought it this morning for fifty cents." Pernie Boyd shows me the stub, but he don't let go of it.

Omer steps up behind me with a wild, colored-boy look on his face, and Pernie throws the raffle ticket into the dirt. "Take it! We don't want it. We ain't got no money. You touch us, and our daddy will have you both swinging on a rope." He looks like he might cry.

The hounds sniff all over the ticket, but I kick them out of the way and take it up and look on the back. "When's the drawing?" I ask.

"This afternoon," Pernie Boyd says.

I put the ticket inside the waistband of my britches.

LaRue smarts off. "Keep the ticket. We'll just get the Colonel to take the four bits out of your uncle's pay." He turns to Pernie Boyd. "Come on."

I'd shoot the smirk off LaRue's face if I had Daddy Shine's gun. But I run my hand down Miss Stoney's mane. "Give her a rest until tomorrow," I say to Pernie Boyd. "You can ride her then, but don't be running up on her until she's sure of you." Pernie Boyd practically darts out of the pasture, with LaRue and Miss Stoney following along.

"You just gave up four bits for a little raffle ticket? And they'll make Daddy Shine pay them back." Omer's thick charcoal fingers coil his whip slow and slide it back into his belt loop.

"They ain't going to tell nobody nothing. Heard LaRue wants the Colonel to think he broke that horse," I say. "Besides, you can't never tell about a raffle. Mama always told I was the luckiest child on earth. Might ride that horse clear to Texas and never look back."

"What if you's to win?" Omer's eyes tear up with joy. "Those boys would soil themselves right there. You could go to Texas and get a big mansion." He runs a rag along his upper lip. "I'd come and visit. I would."

"Could happen," I say.

"Would you really leave and gets out in the world like that? Texas is a long way away from me and Daddy Shine, and we's only family you got. You'd miss ..."

"Can't help it, Omer," I say. "I got promises to keep."

"You better promise to let me come visit you. I could bring you some of that saltwater taffy wrapped in fancy paper from Leiper's store, and we could eat it in the front parlor." Omer grins. "On fine silver dishes. Yes, sir."

"You ain't never had saltwater taffy," I say.

"Don't mean I won't someday," Omer says. "I got me some dreams, too."

"Let's go see about the raffle," I say. I grab up an old stick, and we walk out to the road, past Mama's grave. Spring grass almost fills in the dirt. Mama's body probably ain't nothing but bones now, but I got a lock of her hair and a note that keeps her alive in my heart.

Omer stops for a minute, then punches my arm and grins like a new baby cat. I know he misses my mama. She done held on to him like he was her own the night his mama passed into heaven. *"I ain't your auntie no more. I'm your mama now."*

Omer weren't hardly walking then, but he wailed up n'er an ocean of tears. Now, he's a big tall boy for eleven, and he ain't no crybaby, but sometimes at night I hear him missing my mama. I miss her, too, but I ain't cried a drop. Crying don't change nothing.

Levi's place is but a ramshackle livery stable under two old oak trees. Colonel Dill gossips Levi spied for the Union and took up good with the carpetbaggers after the war, but he never says that to the old man's face. The Colonel's got more opinions than courage.

My raffle number is 23, but I don't say to Levi that I even own a ticket. Might as well keep the proceedings honest. LaRue and Pernie Boyd show up for the drawing, but I put a hex on LaRue with my staring, so that boy don't come around me.

The stallion is strong with straight legs, solid hindquarters, and a jetty black coat, but one eye is clouded over with a thin veil of white. Pernie Boyd never made no mention the horse was half-blind. But the mount seems tough and hardy, with a none too narrow chest. Answers to the name *Good Eye*. I was born with talents for horseflesh and know a one-eyed horse ain't no prize, but the stallion walks unruffled by his blind spot until I can't but take to his stubborn spirit.

Levi stands on a sawed-off tree stump. He wears a fancy waistcoat and a travel-stained linen shirt. His hair hangs in a dirty ponytail down his back, and one of his front teeth has a gold cap next to a rotten yellow stub. "Gentlemen, gentlemen, gentlemen," he says to a dozen or so white men hanging around. He ain't talking to the colored boys and hounds standing in the yard.

"The raffle will proceed momentarily," Levi says. "Please take time to peruse this excellent piece of horseflesh, then add to the whims of fate by purchasing additional tickets—for that mere half dollar or two quarters or five dimes or perhaps fifty copper coins jingling in your pocket, this fine animal could be yours! Lady Luck might be sitting right on your shoulder at this very minute, on this very day waiting for your participation. Imagine, gentlemen, riding this exceptional stallion home." Levi smiles a big gold smile. "Now, no need to push. There are plenty of tickets available."

Some men approach a big wood table where Levi takes

the money and tears off the raffle receipts. A shoddy beaver top hat holds the lucky numbers. The heat of the noon sun settles into the yard. More men join the crowd, and after a half hour of milling around, the men start egging Levi to get to the drawing. The top hat is almost full.

"Gentlefellows, we are ready. Get your tickets now."

I hold my number in my head. I don't even bother to pull the ticket out of my waistband. Omer and I stand on the edge of the crowd; an old dog licks my bare feet. The Dill boys weasel their way right up front. LaRue looks back at me, then looks away quick. That hex is working good.

"Before we get to the drawing, a simple reminder of the rules of this raffle," Levi says. "As you all know, the winner must be standing here amongst us on this fine day of our Lord, April 8, 1876, with the winning ticket presented to myself. So, without further delay ..." He holds the top hat up high and reaches for a ticket.

"Number ..."

Levi fumbles around with the papers, and I say a little prayer to remind God that he might owe me a favor if he thinks about it.

"Nummm-ber ... Hold on, gentlemen, I need my spectacles!" Levi reaches inside his waistcoat for his wire-rims.

The crowd rumbles a little.

"Number ... Nummmmbbbber ... Number 23!"

The Dill boys hoop and holler. "We won! We won!"

Omer steps forward, but I hold him back. His jaw pops.

"We have our winners, gentlemen!" Levi speaks to Pernie Boyd and LaRue. "Step right over here, boys. I just need your ticket."

"Somebody stole it," LaRue yells. "But we won that horse just the same."

A restless flutter moves through the crowd. Omer starts to jump in, but I shake my head. You got to be sly herding white folks. He fingers the coiled whip in his belt.

"Well, that's unfortunate," Levi says. "And a problem for you boys. Got to have the winning ticket before I give over that horse."

"I told you, it got stoled," LaRue says. "But Pernie Boyd's the rightful owner."

"How the ticket get stole?"

Pernie Boyd crosses his arms. "D-d-don't know," he stutters. "D-d-don't remember." He inches over to LaRue.

"You're out of luck, son," Levi says to Pernie Boyd. "I run a clean game, and you got to have the ticket. The rules are the rules."

"Well, I can tell you who stole the ticket!" LaRue points at me. "Prometheus Jones, that's who! That ignorant slave is a no good thief!"

"I ain't no thief, and I ain't no slave!"

Voices echo through the commotion.

"So what is it, boy, you got the ticket?" Levi yells over to me.

I make my way to the wood table, slide my hand under my shirt, and show the ticket to Levi. "Pernie Boyd here gave it to me this morning fair and square for breaking LaRue's filly. I never stole nothing."

"Is that true, son?" Mr. Levi asks Pernie Boyd.

Every pair of eyes in the crowd stares at Pernie Boyd. "I don't remember clear," he says.

I shoot a fierce, hateful look from my eyes and pray for Mama to send devil spirits down on Pernie Boyd. He sucks in his breath, and I watch him work the rabbit's foot in his pocket, rubbing its charms.

"I mean, I don't rightly remember," he says. "Might have ..." The boy acts like he might go to twitching. Mama's magic is powerful.

"Well, what is it?" Levi's patience done run out, but he holds the crowd still with his voice.

"Guess I might have give it to him. ..." Pernie Boyd's voice is puny, hardly a whisper. "Guess that's right."

LaRue don't like the answer. "So you're taking up for that lying slave?"

"I'm as free as you!" I yell at LaRue.

LaRue spits into the dirt. "You got a black temper, slave boy. Far as I can tell, you got nothing in common with a white. You bullied my brother until he gave over his ticket, that's all." LaRue turns to Levi. "Pernie Boyd thought he might get strangled dead if he didn't hand it over."

"Now, son," Levi says. "Your brother gave the ticket away. Stood right here and said so." He turns to the crowd. "Gentlemen, gentlemen, gentlemen, there seems to be a misunderstanding. It appears the ticket was traded for honest work. Prometheus Jones is the rightful holder of the ticket and thereby the raffle winner."

"Just like some Shylock to cheat us out of what's ours." LaRue won't let things alone. "What scheme you cook up with that slave boy?"

"I thought you run an honest raffle, Levi!" a shout says from an unnamed voice in the crowd.

"What about my money? You let that black ninny win!"

"You have this all worked out with that darkie?"

"Stealing the ticket's same as stealing the horse," someone hollers from the back of the crowd. "That rafter would make a right good swing! Yes, siree!" Me and Omer swap glances, and he heads toward the back of the barn.

"That's what I say."

"Hell's fire!"

"Gentlemen, sirs, gentlefellows, please ..." Levi repeats in a loud voice. But this ain't a bunch of gentlemen.

I lean up over a couple of heads and see Omer. He sees me, too. I nod over to the horse.

"I've been running this raffle for two years," Levi's voice booms across the yard, "fair and square. Don't get swayed by this young man's erroneous conclusions."

LaRue jumps up on a wooden barrel and shouts into the crowd. "He ain't nothing but a lying rascal!"

I hand the ticket over to Levi, and we agree with a glance that I need to hightail it out of there. By this time, Omer is untying the stallion.

"We tar and burn double-dealing cheats like you, slave

boy!" LaRue has the crowd jeering. "You and that skulking cousin of yours."

I don't wait around. Omer stands back and lets the horse reins dangle. I run, swing up on the rail, and land on the stallion's back, same time as I reach down for the reins and pull Omer up behind me. I kick Good Eye hard in the ribs.

Angry shouts sing out from a crowd of men led by LaRue. Omer pops his snake whip into them, catching LaRue just under his pretty nose, slicing his lip and nostril open. The boy stumbles into the crowd, then falls back into a pile of old hay and horse manure. Good Eye races across the yard, and Levi's beaver hat gets slapped from the table. Raffle stubs sprinkle the air like fat snowflakes, and like that, we are past the clearing and headed for the woods.

Somebody unloads a pistol into the air, and Good Eye jumps clean over a felled oak tree. I press my toes into the horse's side until the voices are echoes. Me and Omer fly toward home.

"I'll goes with you, Prometheus," Omer yells into my ear. "We can heads west and make our fortune!"

Nobody's in the yard when we ride up. I run into the springhouse, grab my duffle and the money I been saving, then out again. Omer meets me with a shoulder full of rawhide braids, a gunnysack, a scratched canteen, and a smile that shines out of his face like Christmas. "We can take my leatherwork and sell it for cash money," he says.

"But we got to tell Daddy Shine where we headed."

"We do, and we'll see heaven with our own eyes before night," I say. "Come on! We're in a pretty fix, and we ain't got time now. ..." I rush to take up Good Eye's reins.

Omer's smile vanishes into nothing. His chin quivers, too, but he sets his lip to keep it still. "I can't be leaving with no word."

"You done cut a white man, and they're calling me a horse thief! We'll be swinging from that live oak if we don't go now!"

"I can't leave Daddy Shine. ..."

"Your daddy can't fix what we done. He hides us, and they'll be after him, too."

"I can't go."

The barking is louder now. Shouts sound out from the woods. There ain't no time for worry.

"The Dill boys ain't about to forgive and forget," I say. "And I ain't going to let Daddy Shine see you laid out dead at the undertaker's. We'll send word once we get safe."

"Cross your heart and hope to die?"

"I ain't dying yet if I can help it." Horses' hooves ain't far down the road. "Now hurry! Come on."

Omer gathers up his rawhide, jumps on a fence rail, and throws a leg over Good Eye. "I heard the West ain't but one big old desert full of sand. Is Texas like that for sure?"

I give Good Eye a soft thrash of the reins, and we head down the road in a full gallop. "Can't tell," I say. "But we're bound to find out."

“We going to Texas to find us a fortune!” Omer hugs me around the waist. “With a big old mansion with fine silver dishes!”

“I ain’t settling down!” I say. I push my heel into Good Eye’s ribs, and we race for the woods.

“You would if you *had* a mansion.”

But I don’t want no mansion and no silver dishes either. The dust hurries up behind us. Good Eye’s strong, sure legs take us toward the afternoon sun until finally there’s no sound of hounds or horses following. Something good is waiting for me in Texas. Something no mansion can contain.

CHAPTER TWO

Fate steps in on the way to Texas.

"You just going to walk up to a white man cattle boss and ask for a job?" Omer's voice echoes out into the dark. "You don't know nothing about herding cattle. Never ever seen more than a milk cow until today." If Omer would stop talking for about a minute, I would be asleep.

"Do we got a choice?" I ask. "We ain't half on our way to Texas and my saved-up money is down to six bits in the heel of my boot."

Good Eye done carried us west; cross the Mississippi on a steam ferryboat, then through Missouri and Kansas to make camp just outside Dodge City. The town is alive with cardplayers, friendly women, drunks, and restless cowpunchers, all ready to tell you stories and take everthing you got. Me and Omer ship off a telegram to Daddy Shine, trade Omer's fine braided quirts for new boots at the dry goods store, and leave town early.

I pull our blanket tight around my shoulders and close my eyes. The ground is hard with nothing but a thin tarp under us, but I'm bone-tired weary.

"Don't you want to be a cowboy?" I ask.

Omer don't answer. The night air is cold for May; I know Omer feels it, too, because he's backed up as close as he can get next to me, and I can feel his shiver every time the wind kicks up.

"You ain't never even milked a cow." Omer talks loud, like I might be bedded down in a makeshift camp a mile across the prairie. Good Eye snorts soft into the night air. I'm not the only one Omer's disturbing.

"We don't have to milk them, just lead them along a trail," I say. "That ain't hardly nothing."

"Cattle's mean." Omer tugs on the blanket tight.

"I guess. Get enough of them in one spot."

Tell has it that an outfit up from Texas done lost a man in a cattle stampede. They already have a couple of colored boys working for them, so I have in my mind to ride out and see the camp boss first thing in the morning.

"That cattle done stomped that cowboy to death?"

"I guess so. Said he ended up a mess of blood and bones. Not even enough to bury good."

Omer's quiet for a long time. "Prometheus?"

"Yeah?" I don't open my eyes.

"You scared of cattle?"

"No."

"Not even stampeding cattle?"

"No."

"Not even mean, stampeding cattle?"

"No."

"Just wondering." Omer's quiet for a minute. "Prometheus?"

"Yeah?"

"Why do cattle stampede?"

"'Cause certain people talk when they should be sleeping, I reckon." It ain't fair to talk ugly to Omer. He's here because of me. "*You* scared of cattle? Ain't no reason to be scared. I won't let them hurt you."

"Me? I ain't scared!"

"Good. Don't need no nervous cowboys. Besides, you could snap that whip of yours and make all them cattle behave like proper ladies and gentlemen."

"A regular tea party?"

"Nice and fancy. Them cattle probably worried you'll take the job."

I hear Omer's soft laugh. "Well, I'll just let them worry, then. Night, Prometheus."

"Night."

A yawn lets out of me, and the next thing I know the sun is shining right in my eyes, and the wide sky is turning a pale shade of blue. Omer hogs the blanket, so I get on up and find Good Eye waiting for me.

He smells my shirt, and I rub his neck and stand close to his flank. I run my hand across his back, hugging him up as we huddle in his warmth, looking out over this fine piece of country. For a minute I feel Mama watching over us. I pull an old rag of paper out of my hatband.

Andrew Jackson Jones sold off to
Douglas C. Irwin, Negro speculator,
Lavaca County, Texas, in the year of our Lord 1861

Mama had me write it out before she died. I done promised Mama's last breath that I'd hunt for Mr. Jones. She don't tell me exact, but I know Mr. Jones is my pappy. Else she wouldn't name me same as him. Else she wouldn't send me away from Daddy Shine. Mr. Jones is a powerful spirit, and I got to find my way to him.

I hold on to Mama in that full space of morning, but heaven calls her back. I fold the paper neat and slip it into its secret spot in my hatband, then stand close in Good Eye's protection. He turns to me and licks the flat palm of my hand, and I feel luck washing over me.

I don't tell him, but Good Eye owns some of my heart now. I nudge my face into his neck just long enough to breathe in his smell, then kick off Omer's blanket, and we pack up and ride over to the cattle outfit before breakfast.

The camp boss's name is Seamus Beck. He sports a fancy vest with a gold chain, a black derby, and a full, wide mustache curled on the ends like some dandy, but he ain't no fancy man. His face is leather, bronzed and rough, and his eyes got some laughter dancing inside them.

"Men call me Beck," he says, "or a lot worse. Now where might you lads be from?" Beck's voice plays like music.

"Tennessee," I say. Omer and I have already agreed I'll do the talking.

"Spent a night in hell there a dozen years ago, don't you know. November '64," Beck says. "175th Ohio regiment."

"We're looking for work and heard you lost a man," I say. "Name's Prometheus Jones, and this is my cousin, Homer Lovejoy Shine. We call him Omer."

"You got some highfalutin names there," Beck says.

"Mama said they's God-given," I say. "'Cause Omer and me's both got talents. Omer's good with leatherworks and blacksmithing. I'm a hand with horses and got the good eye of a marksman. Can shoot the shine off a crow if the sun's right. Seated my share of wild colts, too. Worked the racehorse stable at Colonel Highram Dill's place near Nashville of late."

"Ever done any cowpoking, have you now?" Beck studies me sharp with eyes the color of summer swamp water. He looks over Good Eye, too.

"Not yet," I say.

Something friendly moves around Beck's stare. "'Em nice new boots there. You're not tenderfoots, are you?"

I shake my head. I know what he means by *tenderfoots*. We ain't no Dill boys. We know how to work.

A wise smile lights up Beck's face, and he hitches up his britches. "Well, I only hire a man if we chew a little fat at the fire, don't you know. So go grab some fry, and we'll have a bit of conversation. Ask for Ole Woman. He's got a beard and a stale cigar, but he'll feed you good as any skirt on the continent. I'll be along shortly."

Ole Woman serves up two plates of biscuits and

potatoes slathered with pepper-dotted gravy. He is a big Negro man with a chewed cigar stub held between two rows of ivory teeth. Omer gulps down chicory coffee and asks for seconds. Ole Woman smiles. I guess he does better cooking than me. They commence talking about the fine details of a fried pork chop.

Beck comes and sits with me, and I ask as many questions as I answer. Beck's outfit is up from Texas with three thousand mixed steers he calls beeves under contract for the United States Government and the Fort Peck Indian Agency.

"Beeves goes to the agency so they can feed the Indians in the winter," Beck says. "If the settlers and miners can't kill the Indians by autumn, the government feels obligated to feed them." Beck pulls a pouch from his pocket and tweaks out a thumb-sized pinch of ground leaves into his kerchief. The leaves give off a sweet smell, stronger than Mama's root tea. "Makes no difference either way. I'm here to deliver cattle and get paid, eh. Indian affairs are not my concern, and they'll not be yours if you plan to work for me, understand?"

"I got nothing against Indians. Ain't even seen one. How soon you headed back to Texas?" I ask.

"No more than two months. This herd will be in Deadwood, Dakota Territory, by July 4, come the devil or daylight, now. I expect work on this outfit, lad, so if you're looking for some adventure ..."

"We know about work."

"I suspect you do." Beck twists the tea tight into the kerchief and stirs it in a tin of hot water. "If things go well, I'll hire you to ride back with us or you can stay north when we deliver the beeves," Beck says. "Can't promise work more than a season, but Texas outfits have an eye for good hands."

We need the money, but two months to Texas? Omer sits with his back to the warm fire, licking the last of the gravy from his soaked fork. I got Omer to think about now. And me, too. But it's a far piece to Texas if you go through Dakota Territory.

Beck shows me a mile of light-colored cattle of good flesh and long legs, all wearing a diamond and dot brand singed out of their backsides. Besides Ole Woman, the crew is eight men and sixty or more horses.

"You know something about horseflesh, do you?" Beck asks.

"Been told I do," I say. Beck exchanges looks with his horse wrangler, and they both grin. I let them laugh.

"Have you now? Want to show us what you got?" Beck nods at his wrangler. "I've got a horse for you."

"I can ride him," I say.

"You might take a look first," the wrangler says, like I ain't got a lick of sense.

"I can ride him," I say.

Beck twirls his mustache for a minute. "If you can ride this frolicsome little beast, you got yourself a job, laddie."

Omer hears Beck's offer, and his eyes get wide and

happy. His smile tells me he could get used to decent cooking. Being a cowboy might not be so bad.

The pen ain't nothing but a rope strung out from the chuck wagon to two stakes pounded into the ground. The wrangler brings up a hobbled mustang that pants angry puffs of air from his nostrils all the while they're saddling him. The minute the hobble ropes are off, he's kicking out dust and backing up against the cinch.

Beck rolls a cigarette. Something in his eyes lets me know he wants my neck in one piece. "You sure you want to do this, lad?" he asks.

I dust my hands in the dirt, and Omer slaps me on the backside. "Do us some good, Prometheus!" Then in a quiet voice he says, "These cowboys say they's a gold rush up in Deadwood. Gold laying rights in the street." He grins. "Get us some mansion money!"

The wrangler watches us, then hands me a worn leather glove. Blue bloodshot eyes squint out from his sun-leathered face. "Since you know everything about horses, I won't tell you this horse has a belly full of bed springs. Mustangs is mean. You think they're getting use to you, and they'll turn around and kill you."

"I know about horses," I say.

"You ain't shy about saying it, so let's see what you got. Wrap the rope around your glove, like this," he says. The muscles in his arms flex hard and full. "If you let go and end up on the ground, that mustang will kick you to the Mississippi. I done cleaned up the mess from one trampled cowboy. I don't need another." The old cowboy folds his hands into a sling, ready for me to step into the saddle, but I ain't ready for that.

I grab the cheek strap and pull the horse's neck toward me. "You got an old feed bag of some kind?" I ask.

"Huh?" he says. He pulls an old burlap square from the wagon and hands it off to me. "Where did you get the wit to know what you're doing?"

I hold the cloth up in front of the mustang's nose and let him breathe it in, then I rub it along the horse's head and over his eyes. I hum a low tune in my throat and hold the mustang's reins close to me so he can get the smell of me.

I nod, and the wrangler offers his sling again. I swing my leg over the mustang's back and ease my foot into the stirrup, checking his temperament. An angry shudder floods out of the animal's flesh, but I pull tighter on the strap, steadying the stirrup before I let go. Once his head is free, the mustang stands quiet, deciding if he wants to toss me to heaven's gate. We both know he ain't ready to give up the fight.

He pitches and kicks and flies off in a flurry of dirt. I buck and toss and fling like an old rag doll, but I don't let go. I push myself sideways out of the saddle a might and stand in one stirrup to keep the jolts from throwing my head back. The rope cuts into my gloved hand, and my shoulder aches with every jerk, but I hold on like me and this old mustang is blood and bone growed together.

Every man in the outfit gathers along the rope, yelling for me. I don't listen to them. I just stick with the horse like I got nothing else in the world to worry about. When I'm covered in dust down to my boots, the horse finally tires out and slows to a trot. The wrangler flips a rope over the mustang's neck in time for me to jump to the ground.

Omer and the whole crew of cowboys collect around me, slap me on the back, and shake my hand. "I told you he could do it," Omer says. "I told you!"

Beck sits on the side of the chuck wagon and blows smoke out in front of him, then twirls the end of his mustache.

"Bully rough riding, son. Prometheus, was it?" he says. "I hope you handle a shooting iron as smart. But you'll have to start at the bottom and let us see your worth. Work is seven days a week until we get to Deadwood. Thirty-dollars-a-month pay for you, twenty dollars for your sidekick. You can draw against your wages and get outfitted in town." He holds out his hand to me. "We leave at sunrise tomorrow."

I take up Beck's hand and shake on our deal.

"You'll be working for the wrangler who gave you the glove," Beck says. "Name's Nack. He's the old man in our party, and a bit sour by nature, but he's strong as a bull and knows horseflesh. You'll learn if you pay attention," Beck says. "Your sidekick can work the wagon with Ole Woman—help with the rigging. Make your introductions here to Big Henry, Tuttle, Con, and Rio, and they'll get you acquainted around to the others. Nack can help you cut your trail horses from the remuda. Cheers to you, lads. Welcome aboard."

By that night, me and Omer are lying with our feet to

the fire, wrapped in tarpaulin and double-blanket bedrolls. We are each the proud owners of canvas shirts, britches, and oiled overcoats. Omer has a new hunting knife, a bag of saltwater taffy, and a dozen long strings of rawhide for braiding. I own a Texas-made saddle, lasso rope, fat dull-rowel spurs, and a .45 Colt pistol. Good Eye has a new pony blanket and a bunch of fresh carrots. I've done closed my eyes for the evening.

"Prometheus?" Omer's voice is a whisper so as not to wake up the other cowboys in camp.

"Yeah?" I say.

"Remember when we was little and played Yankee soldiers against them yellow jackets?" he says.

"Yeah," I say. "I remember."

"I was scared of them hornets. But their sting didn't hurt."

"We whipped up on them. Not a reb-loving yellow jacket left in the quarters."

"Them wasps looked mean, but they weren't nothing," Omer says. "I think them cattle's the same way. They seem more evil than they is."

"Cattle probably real nice once we get to know them," I say.

Omer don't talk for a minute. "Prometheus, we gonna find us some gold in Deadwood?"

"That would be nice—real nice," I say. But life can't get more rich. I'm on my way to my pappy—even if it is the long way around.

CHAPTER THREE

A curious cowboy gives me some news.

"We'll drive to Ogallala, then swing west toward Sidney, then up through Buffalo Gap to Deadwood." Beck does his preaching the next morning at breakfast. "Prometheus, help Nack get the horses going. Rio here will ride drag with you lads to bring up the stragglers."

Rio looks over at me and nods. He's a big Mexican, but he ain't been a full-grown man for long. Still, he has broad shoulders, brunette skin, and dark oiled hair under a wide-brimmed slouch hat. I nod back, but we don't exchange no pleasantries. Omer and that Ole Woman cook are already thicker than thieves, but I ain't anxious to share my trust.

Along with Good Eye, I've got me a string of six good mounts and a pinto not worth the trouble to saddle. Nack don't apologize for the pinto; she's all that's left in the remuda.

"If you're careful with your horses, the pinto will be along for the scenery," Nack says. "A cowman's no value walking."

"I'm careful," I say.

Nack says the men trade mounts every four hours. We make sure the horses get rested and fed before they're called back to their duty.

Beck and Big Henry count the herd, naming out a hundred, then tying off a knot in a tally string until every head is reckoned for. We untie the ground tethers and hold the horses until cattle rolls out a mile or more along the trail. Omer and the chuck wagon are nothing more than a dot, caught up in the waving bluestem grass. The slowest cattle stop to graze one last time, but Rio slaps their rumps with braided rope, and the horses fall in behind.

The sun barely tops the tree line, and already the day is warming up hot. We are on our way to Deadwood. I turn one last time to look south. Ain't no time for regrets now.

"*¡Buenos días, amigo!*" Rio rides up behind me and stays with me on the trail. "Hello, my friend."

"Morning," I say.

"You been in Kansas for a long time?"

"No," I say.

"Where you from?"

"Tennessee of late."

"I knew a Jones from Tennessee once, but he was a *gringo.*"

"No relation, I reckon."

"You still have people in that country?"

"An uncle of sorts. Married to my mama's sister."

"And your mother?"

"Dead."

"Your aunt?"

"Dead."

Rio nods but don't say nothing for a time. "Did you get that Colt in town?"

"Just yesterday."

"Know how to shoot?"

"Got me some practice squirrel hunting. Reckon I know what I'm doing." I pull my ride away from Rio's stallion, but the horse nudges Good Eye and stays with us.

"You know that cattle and Colts are uncertain friends, amigo?"

"How say?"

"It would not be good to shoot your gun unless there is trouble. These cattle are coward little souls, my friend, and an eager trigger can cause panic. Stampeded two days out of Rock Creek. Then south of Red River Station. Then, a day's drive from Dodge City. Our herd is uneasy."

"They're just a bunch of cows. I ain't afraid."

"This is good, my friend. Beeves can wheedle fear out of you, and I don't like a worried man backing me up. Who knows? Perhaps we will have another stampede before we get to the Black Hills. Perhaps we are unlucky, no?"

"I ain't ever been unlucky," I say.

"Ah, you are confident, amigo." Rio rambles on with his questions. "What brings you and your friend west?"

"Work."

"You not see enough work in Tennessee? A freed man has plenty of work, but no pay? That is a problem, no?"

"You ask questions all the time?" I do a cold stare into Rio's eyes.

"Only when I want to know the answers," Rio says. "A man needs to know who rides the last horse."

"No trouble here," I say. "I aim to get to Texas, that's all."

"Ever been to Texas?" Rio asks.

"Not lately."

"Texas is wild and unsettled. You might not find it suits you."

"You born in Texas?" Now it's my turn to ask some questions.

A slow smile slides over Rio's face. "More or less, but my heart still lives in Chihuahua. They say if a man owned hell and Texas, he would rent out Texas and live in hell. Me, I'd take Texas, but I have the will of a mule, my friend."

"Where abouts you from in Texas?"

"Uvalde. West of San Antone."

"Is that near Lavaca County?"

"West. Beck is near there. Many ranchers in Lavaca. Many *vaqueros*."

"Ever been there?"

"Last year. My wife has family there."

"You married?"

"*Sí*," Rio laughs. "But do not tell the ladies in the saloons."

"Ever there during the war?"

"Perhaps. It has been many years. I was only a child."

"Did you meet a man named Irwin?"

"You have a curiosity, my friend."

"Ever met him?"

"Perhaps I know his name."

Thoughts rush around inside my head. Did this Rio fella have a tie to Mr. Jones? "How long you been with Beck?" I ask. I'm more interested now.

"Long enough to know he is a patient man, but beware the anger of patient men, agreed?" Rio turns his horse back toward the herd. "*Adiós*, Prometheus Jones. We will soon know each other well."

I ain't done talking to Rio, but he touches his hat and rides toward a straggler.

Nack motions me over to him. "Just some sociable advice—you can jaw with your pal Rio and all the Mexicans you've a mind. Ole Woman, too," he says. "But get your work done, and don't expect no white cowboys to buddy up and be pardners out here. Stay to yourself and keep your mouth shut, and we'll make it fine."

"I ain't never talked to Rio before this morning," I say. "He ain't my friend."

"Well, neither am I." Nack stares at me until I look away. "But go ahead and get cozy with Rio—be friendly as you like. No one here takes offense at blacks and Mexicans together."

"You got any other advice?"

Nack grins a know-it-all sneer. "Rio's a good enough man on the trail, but he's got a lust for whiskey. You'll find out soon enough."

Nack gives out advice as fast as old Mama Big on Colonel Dill's plantation.

"Rio says the herd's nervous," I say. "That mean they going to stampede again?"

"Rio needs to keep his opinions to hisself. I'd be more worried about Indians if I was you."

"Why's that?"

"They like to stampede herds and take what they can get in the bedlam. They'll be after our horses, our grub, everything." Nack looks down at the Colt tied on my saddle. "You know how to shoot that iron?"

"I got some talents," I say, but Nack looks at me like I'm lying.

"Do tell?" he says. "Better strap it on. Won't be bad till we get past Ogallala. Beck's a smart trail boss. He'll give up a few beeves to keep the peace." Nack pulls up his kerchief, rolls his reins right, and calls over his shoulder. "Just do your work, and remember, we ain't compadres."

Ain't no white man friend to no black man. He think I don't know that? But my mind is full curious about Indians. Do they hate Negroes same as whites?

But my thoughts don't stay on Nack, or the Indians, or even particulars about Texas. The dust from the cattle and horses kicks up, and I wrap my kerchief around my face. I hold steady in the center, pushing the cattle north. Thin clouds melt into a clear china blue sky, and me and Good Eye ride free in the warmed sun.

CHAPTER FOUR

We ride to Nebraska.

"Why, there ain't nothing to this cowboying," Omer says.

I wash the dust out of my face before we head over to sit for supper. We've traveled almost to the Republican River, and the herd is watered and bedded down for the night two miles off the trail near a wide spring.

"Ole Woman says you just got to look after the king steer, and all them other cows just follow right behind. They named him General Custer 'cause that cattle's pretty like the real General Custer. They say he got long curly blond hair."

"The cow?"

"No! General Custer! Ole Woman says General Custer's a sight to see. ..."

"Ole Woman says that, does he?" I say. "He tell you that king steer weighs more than a wagon and is stubborn as Colonel Dill's mule?"

"I'm talking about the man, not the steer! Ole Woman says the General is as fine a man as you would ever lay eyes on. Strong. Pretty looking. Brave as they come. Tougher than a basket of snakes."

"Don't say."

"That's how Ole Woman describes him."

"I still bet on the steer," I say.

Omer hands me my hat. "I ain't saying cowboying's easy work, but we been riding over a week with this outfit and them cattle ain't as cranky as I pictured them, that's all. Plus, Mr. Nack done hired me out to braid him a new quirt."

"That's good, but Nack ain't the boss, and he don't like nothing about colored folks, so don't think different. We got to worry about Beck. If we do a good job, he might hire us to go back to Texas with him. Hear there's lots of work."

"But we won't need to do a lick of work once we find that gold in Deadwood," Omer says.

"Might not hurt to have some other plans," I say. But I smile at Omer's sure faith.

Omer waves me off, and we walk down back to the chuck wagon and to plates of beans and biscuits. The fire is roaring hot, and smoke fills our lungs. I find a spot next to Rio, hoping to steer the camp talk toward Texas.

"With enough whiskey, any *señorita* has charms, no?" Rio sets the round of men to laughing. "Why, it was love at first drink, and the next morning I was a married man. Only my little *esposa* can't bear to be without her mother, so the old woman graces our home. Now I have to drink to forget I am married. ..."

"Or the little lady does!" Nack pipes up and the men laugh again.

Omer sits opposite me next to Ole Woman and joins in the grinning. Rio looks over. "You are not married, Prometheus Jones?"

"I ain't even fourteen. Not old enough to marry," I say. I take a spoonful of beans into my mouth to avoid talking more. Ole Woman gives Omer a wink.

"So you are young, but you have many señoritas in Tennessee?" Rio is playing me to the boys now. I can't say I appreciate it. "You are lucky with women?"

"Plenty of times."

Omer laughs out loud. "Prometheus, you never even kissed a girl."

The boys' laughter spits into the fire.

"Great whale of Joner! We got us an innocent!" Tuttle raises his cup.

"You never been kissed?" Con reaches across and jabs my shoulder. "Not even by your mama?"

I just eat my biscuit and don't say nothing. The men are worse than gossiping women.

"We got us a mission, boys! First thing we get to Deadwood, we're got to find a little girl to give Prometheus Jones here a big sloppy kiss." Tuttle empties his coffee like it's a shot of fine whiskey.

"'Course we might not find a pretty girl!" One of the other men snorts out a laugh, and Omer joins in the merriment until he wipes his eyes on his sleeve.

“*Está bien*, you are young.” Rio scratches the side of his cheek and smiles. “The charms of women will thrill your heart, but take my advice and beware the beautiful señoritas unless you are looking for a wife.”

A couple of the men toast their coffee mugs and vow to find me a kiss. I give Omer a hard look that lets him know he better just keep his mouth shut next time.

Beck throws the last of his tea into the dirt. “You lads' talking talents is a sheer wonder. We'll keep the same night guard starting at dark. Rest well if you can. Tomorrow we'll cross the Republican.” The boys begin to mill about, but Rio stays put.

“Tell me more about Texas,” I say.

“Ah, sweet señoritas in *Tejas*?” Rio smiles. He knows I ain't asking about no romance.

“I want to know more about Lavaca County,” I say. “What do you think of that country? Might want to go down there someday.”

“Then you are headed the wrong direction, amigo,” Rio says.

“How long's Beck been down there? He ain't no Texan.”

“After the war many gringos came. Yankees with money and opportunity, no?”

“Did you say his outfit is from Lavaca?”

“A day's ride from Lavaca. Gonzales. Perhaps if you stay with Beck, you will see. ...”

“A day's ride?”

"Sí."

"A lot of cattle outfits you said?"

"Sí. You have an interest in horses; perhaps you will find prosperity there, Prometheus Jones." Rio smiles. "But first you must experience life on the cattle trail, no?" Rio pulls a small dull-colored flask out of his boot and motions an offer to drink.

I shake my head and Rio shrugs, then turns and takes a nip from the flask.

"Said you knew a man named Irwin?" I ask.

"An old friend, perhaps?"

"Could be."

"It is not the same man, Prometheus Jones. Irwin bought and sold bills of lading—slaves—before the war. He would not be your friend."

"But he might know—" I stop. I don't mean to say so much.

"No, Irwin will not be *amistoso* to a black man. He has no more conscience than a cow in a stampede, Prometheus Jones." Rio stares at me. "You have some business with this man?"

"It's time for my guard," I say.

Rio shrugs, and I gulp down my coffee and turn my grub dishes back in to Ole Woman's wreck pan for washing.

"Now don't be making any trouble with Omer." Ole Woman starts on me right away. "I saw that face you give him. ..."

Omer hides behind the wagon and tries to keep me

from seeing him, but I catch his eye. He holds out salt-water taffy as a peace offering.

"You ain't one minute no innocent, Prometheus," he whispers. "I bet you know everything about talking to ladies. Womenfolk ain't no different than horses."

I take the candy and shake my head at Omer. I can't be angry with him for being a boy. A man knows women got more spirit than horses. Mama done set me straight on that.

I grab up Good Eye's reins and start the mile-long circle around the beeves. The sun is only a glow at the horizon now; a band of darker blue rises up out of the ground. *Douglas C. Irwin, Negro speculator.* He's the man that sold Mr. Jones away from me and Mama. The same man—still in Lavaca.

Big Henry rides on watch with me; me heading to the right, Big Henry to the left, with us making a big loop and passing each other on the far side of the herd. The cattle are tired and mellow from the pace of the day. Mama holds out a lone star twinkling from the sky.

Far off, I hear Tuttle singing by the campfire in a sunny, sweet voice. He ain't singing for us; he's singing to keep the beeves calm and happy.

> *"No chaps, no slicker, and it's pourin' down rain,*
> *And I swear, by gosh, I'll never night-herd again.*
> *"Come a ti-yi yippee yippee yea, yippee yea,*
> *Come a ti-yi yippee yippee yea."*

I've only just passed Big Henry when Beck joins me on my ride.

"C'mere, lad."

I tip my hat. "Evening."

"We're taking the herd across the Republican in the morning, now," Beck says. "The river's no more than about ten rods of swimming, but we don't want to be losing cattle. The man you replaced was a fine swimmer and he and Nack could lead General Custer and the rest of the herd across water easy as Jesus. I see you got a connection with that horse of yours. Think you and Nack could swim across and get that obstinate steer to follow?"

"Might be."

"You know how to swim?"

"I ain't never drowned."

"Good then. You'll give it a go?"

"Yes, sir, I guess I will."

Beck nods again and then rides back toward Big Henry. I can't turn down nothing Beck asks me to do now. Not when he's heading back to Texas and could take me with him. I lean down and sweet-talk low in Good Eye's ear, then rub his neck with the flat of my hand. Good Eye will have to keep both of us afloat. I ain't never learned to swim.

CHAPTER FIVE

Me and Good Eye go for a swim.

"All right, lads, let's get to it." Beck snaps shut his watch. "I'll bring the General around, so stake your claims. Here's your chance to learn the river. Leave your saddles here and the chuck wagon will float them across. Let's get these beeves north before dark." Beck touches the brim of his hat and rides out, with me and Good Eye staring at a quarter-mile band of lapping river water.

Rain upriver has made the current muddy. Nack is already off his mount, stripping out of his boots and dungarees to his long johns.

"Come on. We'll swim across once for practice—see how deep it is," Nack says. "This ain't lollygag swimming—you need to pay attention. Wrap up your clothes in your oilcloth and tie it to your saddle," he says. "That way you won't be wearing soaked britches once we get the beeves across. You'll have to carry your boots over your head."

"How deep is it, you think?" I ask.

"We'll see as we cross. Probably no more than ten or twelve feet. Not deep."

I chant one of Mama's spells into Good Eye's ear, then slide off my saddle and pull off my shirt. The horse will do the swimming now if I can just hold on.

We unload our saddles to a nearby rock, and I start to skin off my undershirt.

"Where'd you get that back?" Nack asks.

I don't answer.

"You run off?"

"No, I got me some learning at the Freedman School, and Colonel Dill's overseer got ill over it. Whipped my back ..."

"You got whipped for going to school?"

"Said schooling wouldn't teach me to do honest work. But it didn't hurt none. Got me a McGuffey Reader out of it." I don't tell him how Mama cried and patted cool water on my back all night. I don't tell him that the next morning me and Mama started saving our pennies and nickels to get to Texas.

"You can read?"

"I can pick out letters better than a lot of folks. Write out *Prometheus Jones* and a bunch of other words."

"Well, I wonder. I never met a darky that could read."

"I told you I got talents. All God-given."

"Then let's see if you and God can swim this horse to the other side." Nack pulls his hat low and mounts his horse bareback, holding the reins in one hand and his boots in the other.

I hold up my .45 to Nack.

"Stick it in your boot," he says. "But next time, leave it in your bedroll or give it to Ole Woman."

I follow him.

"Stay even with me," he says. "But don't crowd. We do this for real, we got to flank the General, and we don't want him spooked by getting too close. Give your horse his head."

We walk the mounts into the water. Good Eye holds up, then steps careful. He don't like the slick rocks of the river bottom. I wish for my rowels to nudge him on, but better to have dry boots, so I press my heel into his side a little ways, and he lurches forward. Even a good horse got to mind.

"Don't pull on the reins. If your horse gets away from you, don't panic. Just hold on to his tail and swim across behind him, but don't let go if you plan to live. Beeves ain't polite swimmers." Nack calls over the splash of the river. "Pay a mind. The General likes to play nervous Nellie, and we can't afford no hesitation on his part. Let your horse set the pace and move the steer across."

Nack pulls his reins to the far side, holds up his boots, and gives his mount a little jab in the ribs. Good Eye follows up to his withers. The water splashes up cold. In a minute, Good Eye is searching for footing, but there ain't none. I let go of the reins and rest my boots on my shoulder, but the horse don't take to the water. The current sprays into his clouded eye, and he jerks back in a panic. I slide my fingers in his mane and push his neck forward gentle-like, then squeeze my knees into his sides to stay with him. I can feel his legs working.

Nack is a good length in front of us now. The current tugs at me, and I shiver from the cold water rushing around my legs and chest. My ears fill with my own breathing and heartbeats, but I don't pay them no mind. I just hold on.

Good Eye pulls to his blind side but stays solid in his swimming, splashing muddy river water in my face and eyes.

We almost make it to the center mark when Nack hollers loud. He thrashes the water and near jumps clean off his mount. His horse twists backward with a splash that smacks Nack hard into the water. Nack and his mount are under! Then I see it. A snake!

I draw my Colt out of my boot and cock the hammer. I spot the snake just under the water, hug my boots to my chest, and squeeze off a shot, just as Nack bobs up with a wide gasp and a splash of river water. Half of the snake flips into the air over his head, and the bullet skips along the top of the current until it sinks into the mud.

"You trying to kill me or the snake?" Nack yells out. "Here! Grab hold my boots!"

I reach, but I can't juggle my Colt and my boots without jinxing my luck for staying afloat. Nack's mount is almost on top of us, and Good Eye gets edgy and splashes up a fury of water until I let go of his mane. He swims strong to stay ahead of Nack's horse, but I can't stay seated with the current, so I grab my Colt and my boots and reach for a handful of horsehair tail and swim behind Good Eye best I can.

Nack's boots tip into the river and sink like toy boats. He yells and starts to swim toward his boots but disappears in his mount's splash. The horse flails the river fast and hard behind me. One kick from that mare, and I'll be lying in a watery grave. I yank Good Eye's tail hard as I know, and the water forces me forward, away from Nack's horse, toward Good Eye's far flank, but muddy river water stings my eyes, and the current starts pushing me back toward the mare again. Nack? Where's Nack?

Nack's horse passes Good Eye in a swirl of foam and fitful kicks. Panic swims alongside her. I can hear her high-pitched squeals and see the bulging whites of her fearful eyes.

Suddenly, the weight of a cotton bale presses on my chest. My arms move slow and heavy, and my heartbeat makes a sweat on my face. I dodge in and out of the horses' kicks, trying to keep clear of their panic. My back is sore and weak. I kick my legs and arms harder and harder to fight the current, but I'm slow as molasses. I can't escape!

Then quick as it happens, Nack's mount finds some footing. Good Eye races right up behind Nack's horse and drags me into chest-deep water. Both horses stomp for solid mud, then settle down to drink like nothing ever happened. I hug tight to my boots and the Colt, pushing through the water for Nack.

Nothing.

I stand still listening to the water.

Nothing.

Then the water hiccups a gurgle twenty yards down the river and Nack's body pops out next to the shore like a hungry catfish. I run down the shallow water to him and struggle to get him ashore. His muscled body is limp as a rag doll. Finally, I wrestle him onto the grass, and a lone boot falls from his grasp. I turn Nack to his side and slap a full blow between the shoulder blades. He grunts, then pukes up river water in a fit of coughing that makes his whole body shiver like a little baby. I'm wet to my bones and shiver right with him.

Finally, Nack takes a long drag of air. "Dang near drown," he whispers, breathing hard. "Why didn't you swim out and grab my boots when I reached out? Why the hell did you ignore me?"

"I killed the snake, didn't I?" I ask. Water drips into my eyes. My hat! I done lost my hat in the river. Somewhere in the current my old hat is floating with Mama's note hidden in the band.

Nack coughs again. "I hate snakes. Cottonmouth devils." He spits into the mud. "Now thanks to you I lost my boot."

"I reached for you, but you was too far gone."

"You get shortchanged on swimming talent?" Nack asks. His voice bites like acid, and we sit cold and angry in our soggy long johns. "How in harmony am I going to ride all the way to Ogallala with one boot?"

“Same way I’ll go without my hat!” I say. My voice is sharp, and Nack don’t say nothing for a long minute. The only sound is our breathing, and the horses drinking in the running river water.

“You ever been bit?” I ask.

“N’er been, but I was reared by a mean older brother.” Nack laughs out a high wheeze. “Been chased with snakes a fair amount.”

I start to laugh but don’t. “I’ll get the horses’ reins,” I say. “Could be your boot and my hat got caught somewhere. I’ll walk down and see if they turn up.”

“I best sit here,” Nack says. “Let my ticker take a breather. Where’d you learn to shoot like that?”

“Eating carrots,” I say. “And I ain’t scared to shoot.” I gather my boots and the Colt and walk down to the horses. I tether them to a tall stand of grass, put on my boots, and hustle on down the bank. My shiny new boots ain’t new no more.

A quarter mile along the river, I see my hat hung up on a tangled tree root on the far shore, but I can’t get to it now. Nack’s boot is done drowned. By the time I get back to the horses, Beck is on the ridge pushing the cattle toward the water. Nack is wearing one boot, untying the horses.

“Hurry up!” Nack says. “We got to swim back and lead them boys over here before they smell this water. You lead.”

We mount the horses bareback and head into the water.

Nack coughs again. "I'm obliged to you for fishing me out," he says. "But if some hellfire snake comes up as we're crossing General Custer, our job is to get that bovine across, understand?" Nack says. "If that steer doubles back, the whole herd will end up at the bottom of the river and us with it."

"You don't want me swimming out for your boots?" My face don't show my smirk, but Nack hears it in my voice.

"Don't smart off to me! This was practice, and you should've swimmed up and took my boots like I asked," Nack says. "But when we got General Custer in the water, nothing matters but that steer. Nothing. Drown if you have to, but that animal gets across."

"I can do my job," I say. "Beck won't have worries from me."

"Well, he won't be happy about my boot, I promise. Beck says a man's nothing in this outfit without his boots and horse, and you owe me a pair of boots. Don't forget that."

Good Eye is shy to the water, and I kick him harder in the ribs than is fair. Nack follows, and pretty soon, we swim across the river back to a spot where some worn rocks give us a hold. I'm better at it this time, but then a snake don't show up this time either. Good Eye shakes off the water, as I wipe the river out of my eyes and suck air into the last space of my lungs. I rub Good Eye between his ears.

Coming up with Beck and two point men, General

Custer leads three thousand cattle down a cut bank to the water. Come nightfall, every one of those beeves will need to be north of the river. A gust of wind whips through the thin cotton of my long johns and I lean in to Good Eye's neck to warm us both.

What Nack don't say is that he'll let me drown lickety-split before he gives up the herd. One cowboy ain't nothing compared to General Custer. So I'll take Nack's advice—any man gets between me and Texas, I'll let him drown.

CHAPTER SIX

I make a pact with Rio, then spy my first Indian.

By dark, the cattle are across the river and bedded down ten miles north, at the far southern edge of Sioux territory. I done made fourteen swims across the Republican since sunup, including one last crossing to find my hat, muddy but not too soaked. Mama's note is safe inside, but the ink is runny now, and I have to look hard to read it.

Finally, we float the wagon across with long ropes and muscle. The work don't go easy, and now even my bones hurt from tired. There's another outfit in front of us, and Beck rides out before supper to hurry them along.

"We won't have our beeves mixing in with theirs," he says, "even if we have to lay off in the morning until they're gone. I won't spend a day cutting cattle if I can prevent the effort."

The land is flat and wide with nary a tree. The grass, tall as new cornstalks, ripples against the wind, except on the trail, where it is matted down into the earth. All around is sky. Miles of sky.

The Sioux land don't look much different here to there,

but Nack says them Indians set a boundary in their eyes that no regular man can see. Says the Indians will kill you for crossing that line, but they'll scalp you dead for your horse, too. Or for your gun. Or good water. Or whiskey. Or a dry pony blanket. Ain't no Indian can be trusted as true. I laugh to my own self: Indians and white men.

We have a heaped-up bowl of bison and beans for supper, as a couple of the boys killed a buffalo and dragged it back to camp. Omer is mighty impressed with the buffalo's size. Neither one of us ever seen so much meat on one animal. With his hunting knife, Ole Woman shows Omer how to sheer off long stretches of flesh to cook over the smoking fire. Now we'll have buffalo steaks and jerky the whole distance to Deadwood.

I sit close to the flame, still trying to get the river chill out of my bones, with my .45 cleaned and loaded in my lap. Figure I might stay heeled with my gun in my belt now that we're so close to Indian country. I ain't scared, but I ain't stupid neither.

"Ready for trouble, Prometheus Jones?" Rio walks over and squats near the fire, pouring fresh coffee into his tin. "I see your Colt is nice and shiny, my friend. Let's hope it stays that way."

"Got wet in the river crossing," I say. "Just drying things out."

"Come on over here and let me take your last dime," Nack yells back to Rio. After working all day with one boot, Nack sits on the opposite end of the camp wagon and soaks his feet in old dishwater, playing freeze-out with Con and Tuttle and a worn deck of cards.

Rio looks at me. "Nack tells me you are an educated man," he says.

"I can read me some."

"Perhaps we can strike a bargain between us, amigo." Rio sits down next to me. His teeth are white against the fire and the night.

"I received a letter from my wife in Dodge City," he says. "I will return the favor to her when we get to Ogallala. Perhaps I could ask after your friend the slave trader, no?"

"I don't know who you're talking about."

Rio looks hard into my eyes.

I speak low. "Irwin?"

"The same."

I don't look away. "You could mention him. But what's the bargain you're after?"

"Ah, this is a delicate matter, my friend."

"I'm listening."

"My wife's people are German, so she does not write out Spanish so well on the paper. She can read English, but sadly I cannot write out the gringo words. So you see, we are fated to be silent across the miles."

"I thought you didn't like being married."

"Ah, Prometheus Jones, marriage is a fine thing. But so are the beautiful señoritas who keep us from being lonely. It is a gift to love women, no? Besides, the boys do not respect a man who is tied to his wife's apron strings."

"You love your wife, then?"

"It is no sorrow to love your wife, my friend. I love her only a little less than my freedom, no?"

"What do you want me to do?"

"Read me her letter. Then let me tell you the words back to her and write them out on a paper so I can post a letter to her in Ogallala. In payment, I will find out about your friend Irwin."

"But ..."

"Ah, this will be our little confidence, my friend. We will wait until the boys are safe in their bedrolls. Then, they will never know I have a tender heart, and you search for a slave trader."

"Wake me up at the end of your watch," I say.

"Agreed." Rio drinks his coffee in one long swallow. "But I must admit to my own curiosity, Prometheus Jones. Why do you have business with this man Irwin?"

A hiss from the fire disturbs the long silence between us. Ashes shoot out like lost stars in the heavens. I shift my weight back from the fire. "Looking for somebody he might know is all."

"A relative?" Rio shrugs. "*No importa,* my friend. But know that Irwin has a hard reputation. If you ask after him, he may come looking for you."

"I guess that would make finding him a might easier, then."

Rio smiles wide and flicks the last of his coffee into the embers. "Until later, then. *Buenas noches.*"

I bed down for the night, but I can't keep my mind from thinking. Omer breathes heavy in a deep sleep, so I sit up and take Mama's paper out of my hat. The words are water-washed into a blur, but I see them clear in my mind ... *Douglas C. Irwin ... Lavaca County ...*

I breathe in and out deep, then I fold the paper, tuck it away, and lean back on the broad seat of my saddle. I stare up at the velveteen sky until my mind settles, my breath falls even, and I sleep.

The next thing I know, Rio shakes my shoulder and motions me near the fading fire. I sit up and put my pants over my long johns, push my boots on, and follow him, rubbing the sleep from my eyes. Braying cattle tells me it's not long until dawn.

Rio don't say a word. He just hands me a thin slip of oilskin paper, and I read the words measured and careful.

"To my beloved husband Reuel,

"I write this letter not knowing when you will receive it. I have some of the best news to write. You are soon to be a papa as I am with child. Mother is worried after my health, as there's been fever among us, but I am well and wait your return. I would be the happiest creature on earth to have your arms around me this night. The moon shines out pretty on the Frio River. God's blessings to you, my husband, and to our new baby yet to be born. Gretta."

Rio ain't listening after he hears the news about being made a papa. He slaps me on the back and grins like a prosperous, rich carpetbagger.

"I will have a sturdy baby boy," Rio says as he folds the paper. "And he will grow into a man like his father."

"This your first?" I asked.

"No, Prometheus Jones. I make many sons."

"How old are you, then?"

"An old man. Almost twenty-three."

"You leave your sons in Texas?"

"Sí. In the small beds of their graves. Luck does not shine on my children, Prometheus Jones. Two sons, twins, both gone to yellow fever. But I am still a betting man."

Rio takes the flask out of his boot and congratulates himself again. Something about him seems young, and all the sudden, I think after Mr. Jones.

Did he forget about me and Mama? Did he forget we was working a field of tired dirt with Daddy Shine and Omer, trying to grow enough turnips and corn and tobacco to give us a home? Only there weren't never enough turnips and corn and tobacco to pay off what we owed Colonel Dill. Mama worked the fields and coughed up the dry clay until the consumption closed her lungs.

"She never told when the baby's coming," I say, but my voice is raspy as a rough-edged rock.

"It will not be long, my friend. Perhaps before we return to Texas." Rio's voice is velvet smooth. "You are happy for me, Prometheus Jones?"

"If you want," I say. I don't turn around. I wipe my nose along the sleeve of my undershirt. "But she might not have a boy. You might end up with a daughter."

"No, it will be a son," Rio says. "It is my fortune. Every man needs a son, and every son needs a father, is that not true, my friend?"

I nod my head, but I don't say nothing. Tears start to gather up in my eyes, so I turn away to wipe my face.

Rio slips the flask back into his boot and hands me a square of oilskin and a stub lead of pencil from his saddlebag. "Let us write my letter," he says. "The camp will be alive soon."

Rio is ready to tell Gretta every cherished detail about his love for her, but he makes do with the words I can write. In a postscript, Rio asks his wife to ask after Douglas C. Irwin of Lavaca County. It's too much to hope for news.

Rio blows on the ink to dry it and puts the notebook in his pocket. "The Ogallala post," he says. He grins one more time. My spirits are better then, and I head back to my bedroll and my dreams.

But I haven't hardly touched my head down to my blanket when Omer shakes me awake. A pale, thin light outlines our shadows, but several of the boys are already stirring from their beds, and Nack sits with his back to the chuck wagon, waiting on morning coffee.

"Prometheus! Prometheus! Wake up! You got to wake up now!"

"Huh? What? Omer ... let me be."

"Look here," Omer says, jerking my arm until I sit up. "Look here on my back!"

Con gives us a shamefaced glance and rubs sleep from his eyes, then draws his pants up over his long johns. Omer don't pay him no mind at all; his voice is excited and worried.

"Look at my back and tell me what you see." Omer twists around and pulls his undershirt up over his head and points to a spot on the inside of his shoulder blade. "The boys said one of them fiddleback spiders done bit me on the back, and I might die!"

"What?"

"A fiddleback spider. Big as a quarter. Right in my bedroll. Nack says they's everywhere in Texas, so it must have sneaked in from the camp box. I felt its sting in my sleep, Prometheus, worse than a yellow jacket. Please, look and see where it bit me. I don't want to die!"

"Omer, I can't see nothing. ..."

"Right on my shoulder. Don't you see it? Nack says I'm poisoned. Come over here by the fire and look. ..."

I wrap my blanket around my middle, then follow Omer over to the extra light of the campfire. Several of the boys are up, waiting on Ole Woman to grind the coffee beans and start up breakfast. Con has his boots on now and sits next to me by the fire.

"Might want to get him on the cure fast as you can," he says to me. "A fiddleback ain't nothing to josh about."

"I can't see no spider bite," I say.

"Probably 'cause he's a colored boy," Tuttle says. "Can't get a clear view on colored skin."

"Needs to start up on that castor oil Ole Woman's got in the sick box," Nack says. He leans forward and spits into the fire. "Let him drink that bottle of castor oil, and the poison will pass right through."

"I ain't drinking a whole bottle of castor oil!" Omer reaches around and tries to scratch at his back.

"Die, then," Nack says. "It ain't no bother to me."

I hold Omer still and look at the space between his shoulder blades. "I don't see no spider bite. Did you see it in your bedroll?"

"Killed it," Omer said. "Beat it to death with my hat."

Tuttle snickers soft under his breath.

"Where is it now?" I ask.

"I gots to believe it's still in my blanket. I didn't see it up close, but I felt it sting me. It hurt like the devil his own self."

I shake out Omer's blanket and look for the spider. Con joins in Tuttle's snorting, and it ain't long before Nack is hooting and clapping his hands. Then all the boys is laughing and slapping each other.

"What?" Omer asks. "What are y'all laughing at?"

I throw the blanket into the dirt. "Ain't no spider, Omer."

"But ..."

"They're making fools of us! You never got bit by no spider."

"But, I felt it. I did. ..." Omer's lip trembles for a second, and then he looks around at me and then at the boys, and a laugh comes out of his throat, high-pitched and nervous. "I knew y'all was funning me," he says. "I's just going along. I knew the whole time." Omer pulls down his shirt and cackles out a big laugh, but I see the hurt in his eyes.

"But you might want to pick on somebody else if you's a mind to keep the peace with me," I yell. I jerk my pants and shirt up and start to get dressed.

The laughing dies into silence. "We was just joshing," Tuttle says after a time. "Don't mean no harm by it."

"Don't know why you're so touchy," Nack says. "We ain't pulling pranks on you. Least your sidekick's got a sense of humor."

Ole Woman comes back to camp with an armful of firewood. "You boys sure up early," he says. "Coffee be on directly."

Con stands up and talks at me. "Keep on and we might think you don't like us," he says. "A little fun's all we was aiming for."

"Don't get mad, Prometheus," Omer says. He grins up wide for all the boys to see. "They think they hoodwinked me, but they never did. Not for a minute. I played right along with them."

I pull on my boots. "Think it's poor to pick on a kid is all." I say loud enough for the whole camp to hear. The sun is a pale rim on the horizon now.

"Ain't you a goody two-shoes." Nack stands up like he's ready for a fight. I'm about to answer him with some harsh words of my own when Big Henry rides up fast to the wagon.

"Indians!" he yells. "We got Indians!"

CHAPTER SEVEN

Pawnee come calling.

Before we can saddle the horses, two Indians appear on a low ridge to the north. The funny thing is, Beck's with them.

"Boss Beck don't look one bit scared," Omer whispers across to me. "You think he done put some powerful trance on those Indians?"

"He ain't no voodoo houngan," I say.

But truth be to God, Beck ain't one bit jittery. He rides easy with a smile on his face.

Gray wolf skins make up the Indians' leggings, and one wears a long dark red scarf wrapped around his head like some woman in the slave quarters. He's bare-chested with red and yellow stripes painted on his skin and a bear-claw necklace standing up like a collar of bones around his neck. A buffalo skin wraps around his shoulders.

The other is young and bald, with a narrow strip of hair greased into a kind of horn. His face is painted white. He wears what looks like an army-issue flannel shirt.

The Indians sit on pony blankets with no saddles and only skin-thong bridles. They ride within the flow of the horses' gait smooth and commanding, but the mustangs' eyes are flat and spiritless. These are work animals, nothing more.

"Prometheus!" Beck shouts out to me as he swings out of his saddle. "You and Big Henry get your mounts ready. We need to cut out a couple of calves for the Pawnee gents here. They'll be scouting for us until Ogallala."

I slip my Colt into my belt and ram my feet into my boots. Omer helps us saddle our mounts, but I watch Beck the whole time. He sits with his back to us, with the Indians facing out toward our view. More than once I catch one of them eyeing our horses.

Nack says ain't no Indian can ever be trusted. I watch the one with the painted face. He smiles and nods and seems right agreeable. But there's no way of knowing what's in an Indian's heart.

They talk to Beck in gestures. The older one runs his hand across his throat, then stretches his ten fingers out as if he's counting. Beck motions something I can't see. The young Indian then points out the sun and moves his arm across a full swing of sky. My gaze follows his hand, but he spots me watching and smiles at me like I'm nothing more than a child.

About the time Big Henry and I are ready to go, Beck motions over to Ole Woman to get the Indians coffee and some buffalo meat, then starts toward us. Nack is up from the commotion, too, moving among the horses.

"What's the trouble?" Nack asks.

"Well, lads, looks like the entertainment is just beginning," Beck says. "Our Pawnee brethren tell me that their enemy the Sioux have decided a little war will keep stampeders out of the Black Hills. Seems the army can't hold back the rush for gold. Buffalo Gap is thick with Sioux raiding parties. There's rumors of scalping from Sidney clear to Custer."

"What's the boys up front say?" Nack wants to know.

"Same story as the Pawnee. Either it's true or a fib made up by the miners to keep out the competition. Give the Pawnee two fit steers, lads, but find ones with sore hooves if you can."

"I'll keep my eye on the remuda," Nack says, looking over at the Pawnee. "Even friendly Indians got ideas."

"Let's get the cattle rolling soon as the grass dries out," Beck says. "The boys up ahead are pulling out this morning. I don't want to mix with them, but we could benefit by hanging close."

Big Henry and I rope out two unwilling calves. We make it back to camp about the time Ole Woman and Omer are packing up the wagon. Looks like breakfast weren't nothing more than coffee and jerky. I take the steers and head over to the chuck wagon. Beck is already gone, working at the head of the herd, and Big Henry rides out to join him.

I hand the ropes of the steers to the young Indian, but he don't take the braided hemp. He stares at me, then wipes his finger along my cheek and looks to see if I'm painted same as him, only black.

I rub the white paint on his face, and it comes off a faint powder on my fingers.

Ole Woman watches us. "That white paint is good luck to Pawnee scouts," he says. "Don't mess with that."

I smile and nod. The Indian takes the rope and smiles back at me like I'm some traveling-show curiosity. His eyelids are tipped in bright red, plucked clean of lashes, and stand out severe from his white face, but he don't seem sullen or hateful like them Johnny Reb soldiers after the war. I don't see no evil omen in his eyes.

Beck is generous to a fault. One of the Indian's mustangs staggers from the pack weight of the buffalo hide and meat from last night's kill. The calves are bawling now, tugging at the ropes. I help the Indian tie one of the calf ropes to the mustang, then talk low into the horse's ear to calm him.

The Indian watches me; then still smiling, he pulls out his jackknife and guts out the other calf at our feet, splashing blood into the mud and the water bucket. He routs around with his knife and pulls out a quivering slug, liver steaming from the warmth of the dead calf in the cool morning. He takes a bite like he's eating an apple in Colonel Dill's orchard, and then passes it to the other Indian. Their bloody grins show their pleasure in the meat.

I look away with a sick feeling in my stomach, but the first Indian takes back the dark red organ of meat and nods to me. He offers it over to me as breakfast.

Ole Woman and Omer stand behind him. Omer's eyes are bigger than Ole Woman's grub plates.

"You got to eat it now," Ole Woman says. "They don't like it if you snub their hospitality."

"I ain't hungry," I say.

"Don't matter," Ole Woman says. "The liver is an offer of friendship. You got to eat it, unless you plan to kill them."

"I ain't wanting to kill anybody," I say.

"Well, you best enjoy, then," Ole Woman says.

The steam from the liver fills up my nose with the sweet stink of blood. I look hard at the faces of the Pawnee. Behind the smears of blood, their faces give out a readiness that's full of spirit and joy, not much different from Mama's look when she departed for heaven. I ain't never seen that look in a white man's eyes.

My hands shake noticeable, but I reach for the liver, and the young Indian lays the warm, black-red mound into my palms. Blood stains my fingers, and I feel Mama's breath on the back of my neck; her sway nudges at me from the divine. *Courage.*

I lick my lips and bite down into the raw liver and taste the blood in my teeth. The meat is thick and slippery and slides down my throat without me chewing. I swallow hard. I wish for some of Omer's saltwater taffy to take the stench of cow guts out of my nose and throat. I pass the liver back to the Indian and don't let my face show the queasy feeling in my stomach. There is respect in the Indian's eyes now.

He lets out a whoop, then the other one joins in and throws the carcass of the dead calf onto the back of his pony, and they ride out of camp with blood streaming down the barrel of the horse. I watch them go.

Ole Woman throws down the butt of his smoke. "Well, don't that beat heck," he mutters under his breath. "You're part Pawnee to them now."

I wash my hands and face in the water bucket, then pour the water into the dirt. Omer watches me the whole time.

"Prometheus?"

"Yeah?"

"You ain't never going to get a girl to kiss you now."

"Not likely, I reckon."

Omer grins. "You want some coffee with your breakfast?"

"Later," I say.

"You ain't scared of them Indians, are you?"

"Naw. I'm thinking they might be like them yellow jackets."

For a minute Omer looks like he don't believe me. "Ain't do no good to be scared," I say.

Ole Woman overhears us. "You ain't met no Sioux yet," he says. "They hate the Pawnee. They won't be offering up liver for breakfast, unless it's yours. Let's get packed up and out of here."

I ride to find Nack. A trampled greensward marks the cattle's trail a half mile down the flats. I find him talking with Beck and Rio.

"Don't let the stragglers wander too far behind," Beck says. "This herd is nervous already, so we need to ride smart, gentlemen. Once we pass Ogallala, the Sioux will be watching for us to offer up a feckless moment. We'll lose it all if they stampede the herd, lads. The scouts will watch with us until we make the Platte."

"Why is the Pawnee so friendly?" I ask. "We bringing these beeves to the agency for them?"

"Not at all, my friend," Rio says. "This herd will end up in the bellies of Sioux."

"But the Sioux and Pawnee don't—"

"Things are never what they seem, Prometheus Jones. Agreed?" Rio's horse prances on toward the herd.

"Our beeves are a bit of diplomacy, sir," Beck joins in. "The U.S. Government hopes to bribe the Sioux to stay on their lands by giving them food. Our job is to deliver the herd. That's it," Beck says. "So if the scouts can help us, so be it. Besides, don't be getting sentimental, now. These Pawnee expect to be paid in beeves and buffalo. They're not working for love or loyalty."

"What happens if the Pawnee find out about the cattle going to the Sioux? Won't they hate us?" I asks.

"It doesn't matter," Beck says. "The Pawnee already surrendered to the government. They'll do as they're told."

"I never met an Indian I ever liked, Pawnee or Sioux." Nack's voice is hard and dry. "Can't trust the lot of them. The Pawnee lust after our ponies and our chuck. The Sioux want our scalps," he says as he turns to me. "You best keep that Colt handy. We'll hobble the horses at night till we make town."

I don't say about my breakfast with the Pawnee. Figure Ole Woman will report to Beck soon enough.

Nack rides the line with Beck.

"You think the Pawnee will turn on us?" I ask Rio.

"What good will it do them? Beck will be generous and buy their loyalty as long as they work for us. "*No te preocupes*, Prometheus Jones."

"It's just ... Texas ..."

"Ah, Tejas. We will post the letter in Ogallala, my friend. It will not be long. Until then, we will watch with careful eyes, no?"

The dust rises up behind the herd. Rio stares at me until I nod my head, then he smiles, touches his hat, and rides off to the left of the trail.

The rich smells of manure and prairie press into my lungs. The grass in the morning breeze makes a ripple of silk all the way to the sky. My stomach rumbles a wild growl of freedom, and I holler and wave at a small knot of five or six cattle hanging on the trail behind the herd. Good Eye chases them until they get moving.

The raw taste of iron hangs onto my tongue, and I think on them Pawnee boys. They're nothing to Beck, but something about them pulls fierce on my heart. "Ole Woman says I'm one of them now," I say aloud. "Think I got some Pawnee blood in me, Good Eye?"

Good Eye don't answer.

CHAPTER EIGHT

The herd takes a run.

We don't tarry heading north, passing Stinking Water Creek without so much as a howdy-do. It drizzles rain the last thirty miles to the South Platte, so the herd don't plague us none. By the time we make camp by the river, Ole Woman has tattled to all the boys about me and the Pawnee having breakfast. Only Nack takes to razzin' me. Beck don't say nothing.

"I hear that blacks and reds come from the same ilk," Nack says. "That what makes you so good with the horses?" He oils the handle of his new quirt and tests its snap, approving of Omer's handiwork.

"Can't say about the horses," I offer back. "But I ain't got no Indian in me, if that's what you're asking." I pull the hobble rope snug on Beck's roan and work down the line.

"You know that for sure?"

"For sure as I know. I got no knowledge of my people past my mama."

"Where's she?"

"Dead," I say.

Nack don't ask no more questions. He helps me lace the ropes through the rest of the horses' legs until they stand in a long line. I keep Good Eye free and brush down his mane. Nack goes back to messing with his quirt and don't see me sneak Good Eye a pocketful of oats I borrowed from Ole Woman.

Although the rain has stopped, the South Platte is wide and wet, with a gumbo of clay mud banding each side of the river. Beck says when the sand is dry this river ain't nothing more than an alkali flat, so no use risking the beeves to make the crossing now.

"The herd gets stopped in that muck, we'll be taking scatter guns to all of them," Beck says. "Once they're stuck, we'll not get them free." So we set to lay up and let the sun do her business. On the edge of the horizon we can see Ogallala's rooftops. Every cowboy in the outfit is wishing for town.

After talking with the Pawnee, Beck agrees on camp a mile back from the river in a little tangle of underbrush even though he don't like us penned up so close to the bog. We ride the herd to bed ground on a narrow divide behind camp and the river. We'll keep our night horses saddled, ride double-watch, and hope the herd will stay peaceful for the night.

With good sun, we'll be able to walk through the muck and haul water for the horses and cattle tomorrow, then cross after nooning here two days. We'll rest a piece in

Ogallala. Rio can post his letter, and I'll hope for some news about Irwin.

"I'll take the first watch," Nack says, "but don't be late when it comes your time to nighthawk."

I don't grudge Nack his sorry humor. Figure he's aggravated by the holdup of the herd and a tender heel. He's wearing two thick socks on his left foot and is itching for a new pair of boots. Only the dry goods store in Ogallala can set him happy again.

Nack expected Beck to get me to pay for his boots, but when he asked, Beck wouldn't have none of it. "A man takes care of himself" was Beck's only answer. He and Nack ended up crossways, and Nack set to shouting. Beck didn't like that one minute. Now all they make is polite conversation, and I can see Nack harbors a river of spite against me.

I walk back to the chuck wagon. The Pawnee bed down a mile out from us. They done delivered their buffalo and beeves somewhere, so their mustangs roam free along the edge of their camp between me and their fire, like them silhouette pictures Mistress Dill once cut from black paper.

"Got me some son-of-a-gun stew cooking up right here, Boss Beck," Omer says. "We didn't give those Pawnee scouts all the good parts of Mr. Buffalo, no sir! We got liver, tongue, and brains, all mixed with a mess of beans and onions and potatoes. Ole Woman let me do the cooking tonight, and I done my best to makes a lip-smacking meal, so come get it."

Ole Woman laughs, and Omer spoons up a plate of grub for Beck. "Good eats here," Omer says.

Beck smiles and takes a tin of stew, then pours himself a cup of hot water.

Omer hands me a plate, too. "I know you going to like this, Prometheus! I just hope I ain't cooked it too much for you." Omer laughs none too shy, and I see Rio and some of the other boys nudging each other like little children with a secret.

"Y'all gets to eating, now," Omer says. "Before those Pawnee come over and makes themselves at home." Omer dishes out grub, a mound of stew and hardtack, and settles himself between me and Rio, balancing his plate in the circle of his lap. "Boss Beck, you ever kill any Indians?" Omer asks.

"Don't make idle chatter of killing a man, lad, Indian or no," Beck says. He sets to measuring out his tea in his kerchief. "I've never killed a man that didn't grant me permission in some fashion or another."

"They ask to die?" Omer tucks his apron up around his neck and starts in on his stew.

"In a manner of speaking. In my experience, a man's actions talk for him louder than he can himself." Beck opens his kerchief and tosses the ball of wet tea into the fire. It hisses and burns out.

The sky is a perfect clear night, and the dark hugs our backs. The North Star twinkles bright as a jewel on the Little Dipper's handle, and the moon sits like a coin on the horizon. Beeves bellow across the flat, restless and lonesome. One of the boys on watch sings out to the herd, and his voice catches up on the wind. An eerie chill settles in my stomach until I'm as twitchy as the beeves. I set my plate on the dirt and watch the Pawnee fire.

Omer licks the back of his spoon and sops a piece of biscuit around his plate. "But if they ask for it, shouldn't a man take pride in giving them what they want? If somebody's looking for trouble, I'd be pleased as punch to help them find it."

"You're a fighting man, then, lad?" Beck asks.

"Might be. Daddy Shine always says you got to work out your vengeance best you can. Sometimes, I reckon you got to kill somebody for their own good."

Rio grins over at me as he questions Omer. "You plan on saving the Indians, then, my friend?"

Omer talks with his mouth full now. "If we get in an Indian hunt, my knife is sharped up ready, and I got my whip oiled, too. I'll slice them boys into Indian stew!"

One of the Pawnee walks toward the wagon.

I nudge Omer in the side to hush, but he keeps talking. "I'll sneak up on them and slit their Indian throats. They ain't about to get my scalp. No sir! My hair is staying right on my ..."

Something changes in Beck's face. He leans into the fire and points with the edge of his fork. "Catch yourself, boy," he says in a soft tone.

Omer don't stop. "... my little head. Them Indians want

to kill us just because we're going to Deadwood, but we ain't hurting them none. Hear tell it, Indians don't want that gold anyway. And as for me, I could stand a little gold dust in my pocket, I could, and then I's—"

Beck's voice booms out. "Boy, you need to hush!"

I reach over and lay my hand on Omer's arm, but Beck ain't done.

"You're wearing yourself thin!"

Omer stops, looks at Beck, then searches the faces around the fire. "Boss?" he says. "I was just funning ... talking fancy ... I didn't mean—"

Ole Woman puts his finger to his lips. Dry wood snaps in the fire.

"Your stew is a tad tart for my taste, Mr. Shine," Beck says and hands his dish to Ole Woman, then walks out to meet the scout halfway between the camps.

I hope I'm the only one to see Omer's chin quivering. He looks down at his plate and don't say nothing else. Ain't no talk after that from any cowboy. We eat our supper like we're all sitting in a Sunday-school meeting.

Beck comes back to our fire and speaks quiet. The music in his voice is gone. "Our job is to deliver this herd, gentlemen," he says. "That is all we are here to do. We'll fight the Indians if they insist, but I'll take the liberty of asking Mr. Shine to hold his opinions of Indian killing to himself. That includes the rest of you, and I'll take it up with the boys on watch. The United States Government is not paying us to fight the Sioux—so let's keep to our business."

Cowboy hats nod around the fire, but nobody looks up.

Beck waits for a spell, then smiles. “Besides, lads, we’ve got Prometheus here with us as our lucky charm. He befriended our Pawnee brethren. Perhaps he can work his magic with the Sioux, and we all dance a jig through the Black Hills.” Beck chuckles like something is funny, but he don’t find no takers to join him. “God to you on watch, lads. Good night, then,” he says.

Me and Rio sit with Omer until the last man turns in for the night. Rio rolls a cigarette and blows the smoke into the fire.

Omer finally whispers to me, “Think Boss Beck gonna turn me out for my big mouth?”

“He’s heated about being stuck out here’s all,” I say. “We’ll head on tomorrow.”

“Think?”

“Pret near positive.”

“You ain’t for sure? What if he don’t want me on the trail going north? How we gonna get to Deadwood and get our mansion?”

“You’re a worry wart,” I say.

“How’s we going get Daddy Shine out here?”

“We’ll get back on the trail. Beck’ll forget all about it.”

“You think Daddy Shine misses us too much?”

“Not too much.”

“Prometheus, I miss our home place. Can’t help but worry over Daddy Shine.”

"Rightly so. Every daddy needs a son, and every son needs a daddy, I reckon." I look over at Rio. "But we going to get us to Deadwood, and everthing will turn out."

"You think so?"

"All except one thing."

"What's that?"

"Your cooking," I say.

"What?"

"Your cooking is terrible."

"I agree, my friend." Rio grins wide at Omer. "Your son-of-a-gun stew sticks to my ribs, but that is the trouble, amigo. It sticks and sticks and sticks." Rio gives off a loud burp. I cuff Omer in the arm, and a slow, long smile comes up on his lips.

"Prometheus?" Omer says. "I ain't really going to kill me no Indians."

"I know."

"I'll tells you a secret," he says. He leans toward me. "I'm scared of Indians—even them Pawnee. They stare right back at Beck with their wild eyes when he's talking to them. Don't even look away for a minute. Scares me, but don't tell nobody I'm a sissy."

Omer ain't no sooner confesses his fear than the shrill of a howl pierces the dark. Across the flat, the Pawnee jump to their horses and the ground roars up in a din of thunder getting louder and louder. Rio throws his cigarette into the fire. The Pawnee shout across to the camp in words I can't understand. Over the shriek of horses and the holler of cowboys, Beck's voice bellows out as loud as the beeves. "Get to your horses, lads! Run! Buffalo coming!"

Ole Woman's pots and pans clatter into the fire. Omer is shaking worse than the ground. I push him up under the camp wagon and try to stand up, but the ground throws me back.

"*¡Rápido!*" Rio shouts at me. "Get to your horse!"

I stumble to Good Eye and swing into the saddle. Within a minute, the pounding of a hundred buffalo hooves shatter my ears. The stampede is running through our camp, right between the river and the herd!

I try to turn Good Eye toward the remuda, but there's no working up the current of racing buffalo to find Nack. Not a slim space of trail separates the snorting, huffing animals. Their huge bodies run close, hunkered down with heads low and tongues hanging pink and wet.

Rio shouts, "Stay close to me. Beck's trying to turn the buffalo south. Keep the herd out of the river."

But there's no breaking free. The beeves make an onrush to join the buffalo, and me and Good Eye swirl along in a mass of hooves and horns.

Rio takes out his Colt and shoots wild into the air, pushing his horse into the flood of the stampede, riding at a full gallop, driving away from the river. I follow, but we might as well be shooting popguns.

Good Eye don't like the roar of the Colt, so I rein him in against a full-sized buffalo centered in a pack of bison heifers, hoping to break the line. The old brute buffalo pushes against Good Eye, running the trail full speed until finally Good Eye falls back.

The moon hides behind a string of clouds. I try again, kicking the rowel of my spur into the buffalo's rib and nudging him to turn. If he turns, the stampede might slow enough to get the bison moving away from the herd. But Good Eye is blinded by the dark and his milky vision and can't see the buffalo running right beside him. He's too timid to keep up, even though I slap his rump with the tails of his reins to keep him moving. Good Eye veers to the right, into a stream of scared cattle.

I pull the reins hard to the left, but Good Eye rears up and the muscles in his neck are tight as fiddle strings. The beeves crowd us in closer and closer. Good Eye turns in a circle, and I lean into him, humming out vibrations from my body, but he's panicked more than I can calm him. I jerk at his reins, but the moon shows herself, and a line of clear path appears. Suddenly, Good Eye bolts toward the river, catching me unexpected. I hit the ground hard, and the night flies up into a thousand broken stars.

I struggle to stand up but can't see nothing in the dirt and the dark. I hear them before I can see good. The blazing eyes of a dozen buffalo coming right for me! There ain't nowhere to run. The eyes are hunting me down, and in a minute I'll be a mess of flattened flesh. The pounding gets louder and louder and louder until there ain't nothing in my head but the rhythm of the hooves and my own heartbeat. Dirt is thick in the air, and the ground shakes harder and harder and harder. I can feel the heat of the buffalo rising up toward me. Ain't nothing to do. Ain't nothing to do but run.

But I ain't going to die cowering in the mud. I run right toward them buffalo, shouting out as loud as my lungs can sing. If I can grab hold of some woolly hide and hang on, I will. Otherwise, I'll pass through the crossroads and meet Mama on the far side of heaven. So I take off running, and the buffalo is coming at me, and I'm running, and I'm running, and I'm running!

But just as I feel the hot breath of the buffalo's tongue on me, out of the dark, an arrow shoots straight into the first buffalo's eye. Blood explodes from his eye socket, and he makes a low groan and veers off toward the river. One of them Pawnee rides up and jerks me onto the back of his mustang. Another buffalo rushes past us into the moonlit dark. The Pawnee howls into the clamor of the stampeding hooves and looks back at me with his painted white face and a flash of smile. The halo of a Zanj angel shines around him.

A pain sets to pounding in my head, but I hold on tight to the rough wool of the Indian's army shirt. The Pawnee crowds his mustang into the sides of the stampeding herd, pushing them away from us. The mustang shudders, but the Indian don't let up. The full power of his body guides the horse. There ain't no rein between them.

I worry for Good Eye, but there's no seeing him in the

dark and disarray. For the better part of an hour, we ride at a hurried pace, pushing the beeves and the buffalo away from the soft mud of the river until Beck gets the stampede turned south, and Rio rides back to tell us to let them run.

"Where is your horse, my friend?" Rio questions me.

"Gone," I say. I jump off the back of the mustang, and I can feel the Pawnee's stare without looking at him. "Back a few miles if I'm lucky."

"The horseman's horse throws him in the dust?" Rio's teeth shine out in the dark.

"Horse panicked is all. I got to go back and find him."

The Pawnee makes a few signs with his hands to Rio, then points to me and yells out, "*Chaticks-si-Chaticks*! *Chaticks-si-Chaticks*!"

Rio whistles low under his breath. "Says you ran toward the buffalo? Calls you brave as *Chaticks-si-Chaticks*."

"What's that mean?" I ask.

"Men of men," Rio says. "It is how the Pawnee call themselves. He honors your bravery, Prometheus Jones. Pawnee respect brave men."

"Guess I got a good angel watching over me." Me and the Pawnee nod to each other as he rides out toward the dead carcass of the downed buffalo. I watch him go for a minute, and I can feel the flesh pricking up on my arms.

"Good fortune smiles on you, my friend," Rio says. "It is good to know a lucky man."

I feel fate's good heart shining down on me from heaven. Mama sent that Pawnee to spare my life.

Rio offers to round up Good Eye, but I don't take his help. I walk back in the moonlight alone. Good Eye is scared, I know. I got to find him. And Omer, too. It's dead quiet now, with just the pain in my head, the matted grass, and the cut-up mud as the only relics of the stampede. We'll be hunting down beeves at first light of day.

I hear a low whimper down a shallow ravine not far from what's left of our camp and mouth a little prayer that it's not Good Eye. It isn't. In a line of low weeds, Nack is lying with his quirt in his hand and his foot bent back in a bloody jumble of torn wool socks. His foot is crushed. He won't need new boots now.

CHAPTER NINE

Good Eye travels the crossroads.

Nack cusses out a slew of not-so-Sunday words between his whimpering. I head fast to the camp for help. A rim of daylight is just making the horizon. Coffee is already boiling on the fire, and Ole Woman and Omer are cleaning up the scattered cookware and bedrolls.

Good Eye is pulled up by the chuck wagon, splashed over in mud. I hurry to him, but I know from the hard line of his muscles it ain't good. My saddle hangs n'er sideways on his back, and he's holding his hoof in the air.

Omer runs out to meet me, and his face is shiny from the heat of the fire. The light catches in his eyes, and I see his worry.

"Prometheus, we was wondering about you!" he says. "Good Eye's hurt. I tried to check his hoof, but he won't let me near him. Can't coax him out of that spot, neither. Snaps big angry teeth at me ..."

I lay my hands on the horse's neck, and a low shudder vibrates out of Good Eye's chest. His heart hammers against my hand.

Omer don't stop talking. "We was thinking the worst 'fore you got here. Not really the worst—I know you're good with horseflesh. You'll probably make Good Eye right as new, I know it. But we was considering the worst, and it's sure lucky you showed up."

"Where is everybody?" Ole Woman wants to know.

I talk low but keep my hand on Good Eye. "Halfway across the flat, hunting beeves, I reckon. Won't know exactly till morning. But Nack's in trouble with a hurt foot. Looks bad."

"Where? What happened?" Ole Woman throws off his apron.

"About a mile down the river. Found him that way," I say. "Don't know what got him."

Omer searches the mess of the wagon for a sturdy length of pole, and he and Ole Woman commence making a rough triangle sling to haul Nack back to camp. They get everthing tied and ready behind one of the wagon mules, then Ole Woman hands me a small flat bottle of copper-colored liquor.

"Pure grain whiskey," he says. "You need a drink before you deal with that horse?"

"Naw," I say. "Get on down to Nack. I'll be all right."

It's a little spell of time before Good Eye trusts me enough to let me check his leg. I slip the latigo loose from the cinch and ease off my saddle, then run my hand down his muddy foreleg and knee. Mud is caked in his hoof, and I try to work it out. His ears lie flat by his head, nostrils working hard and fast. I hum out a low-pitched song and let go of working the mud. Good Eye quiets some. I seen enough of Colonel Dill's racehorses to know the truth in my heart. Good Eye done fractured his leg.

I rub his neck, then rout through the chuck wagon and find a half-rotten carrot. It ain't good, but it's the best I can offer up. Good Eye pushes at the carrot with his nose, but he don't take it from my hand. He stands quiet and waits for me to take care of him. Only there's nothing I can do now. He must've run into the gumbo and got stuck, then panicked and snapped his leg trying to get free. It's my fault for setting Good Eye up against that buffalo. My fault for pushing him too hard. My fault for not taking care.

I know what I got to do, but I stare into the fire until Ole Woman and Omer get Nack carried back to camp. Nack's passed out. Ole Woman says his ankle is broke, and I can see Nack's foot is nothing more than ground flesh below the ankle bone. Ole Woman cleans it up best he can and wraps a clean roll of cotton around it.

Omer sits next to me. "Prometheus?"

"Yeah?"

"Good Eye going to be okay?"

"Nope. Leg's broke."

"Can't you wrap it and put on some liniment like you did for Colonel Dill's horses?"

"It's not a sprain."

"What do you mean?" Omer's voice is nothing more than a whisper.

"His leg's broke." My voice cracks into a harsh grief.

"But you can't—"

"Snapped just below the knee."

"But you know everything about horses. You can fix Good Eye good as new. You know you can."

"It's a bad break. I can't fix it."

"Yes, you can! Make one of them splints and wrap up his leg. You know how to do that. You know everything. You got talents with horseflesh. You can get Good Eye well. I know you can." Omer's voice is all jittery, like he's about to cry.

"I can't!" I shout. "It's a sure break. He's already suffering."

"But you got to try. ..." Omer's voice blubbers out of his crying. "You won that horse fair and square, and he rode us all the way out here. You love that horse. I know you do."

"Omer ..."

"Boss Beck will help. He likes you, Prometheus. He says you're our lucky charm."

"I can't, Omer! Don't you hear what I say? Can't you understand? Good Eye's leg is bad broke, and it's my fault! I ain't lucky! He rode us out here and took care of us, and was as good a horse as a man could have. I done got reckless, and it's my fault! It's all my fault!" Pain sets up in my head like a twisted knife. I rip the Colt .45 out of my belt and hold it behind me until I'm standing in front of Good Eye's blind side, and he can't see me. "I can shoot the shine off a crow if the sun's right! Want to see me?" I yell at Omer.

"No, Prometheus! No! You're still lucky! You know

everything about horses. ..." Omer shakes with sobs. "You can make him right! I know you can!"

I lay the barrel right up to Good Eye's forehead, and I close my eyes and I breathe in the smell of him, and I flick back the hammer quick, and I hold my breath. The pain in my head pounds behind my eyes. I tell myself to squeeze the trigger. Just pull the trigger. Pull the trigger! Pull the trigger!

But I can't.

"It's my fault," I whisper. And I put all my mind to it. But my finger's froze, and I can't do it. I squat to the ground, and Good Eye smells me, and nudges my shoulder. And I sit there squatted in my boots until Ole Woman comes and takes the Colt out of my hand.

"Don't got to think of it now," he says.

Omer cries by the fire for a good long spell. Ole Woman sits with me, but there's such a big empty space in my heart, I can't even feel the grieving.

Finally, Ole Woman stands and wipes his hands on his apron. "Walk back down the river to where you found Nack," he says to me. "Might find the remuda not far. Go on now. Work will keep you from yourself for a while."

I nod. Ole Woman tends Nack, and Omer begins collecting up firewood. Neither one of us speaks. I slip my Colt back into my belt and head down the trail.

Sure enough, not a mile from where I found Nack, the hobble's got the remuda wound tight together in a stand of sumac. I lasso their necks one by one and cut them out. It takes me the better part of the morning to get them freed. By the time I get the horses to camp, Beck is back, looking for fresh mounts and shouting orders.

Beck pulls a thick quirt from his rumpled bedroll and saddles his day mount. "My condolences for your horse," he says. "I took the liberty of taking care of business. We can't be sentimental about these things, eh?"

Good Eye's missing from the spot where I left him. "Where is he? What'd you do?"

"Don't dwell on it, lad. It's done," Beck says. "I looked at the leg; there was no choice. I wouldn't have bet on a half-blind horse in a stampede anyway."

My chest squeezes my lungs until I gasp for breath like an old man.

"You're the outfit's wrangler now," Beck says without ceremony. He don't wait for an answer.

Beck, Rio, and the rest of the boys ride out. I don't ask Ole Woman and Omer about Beck's shooting Good Eye. I can tell from the slump in Omer's shoulders that I won't find no comfort between us.

I find me a tin of hot coffee and look in on Nack. He's pale, and fresh blood soaks his cotton binding, but he's awake—drunk as a skunk, too, shouting out oaths.

My body is aching for sleep, but I saddle a sturdy sorrel from my string in the remuda and grab up the pails to water the horses.

It's long after dark before the herd is bedded down again. Beck says it's a blessing that we've lost only half a dozen beeves. Everyone is fit for sleep, so there's not much talk while we eat our chuck. It's just me and Beck by the time the fire gets low.

"You trust me to be the wrangler?" I ask. "I done lost my own horse. Figured you'd want—"

"With Nack laid up, I don't have much of a choice now, do I?" Beck says. "The Pawnee left out this morning, so half the boys think they had a hand in the stampede. If they show back up, you might distance yourself a bit, and keep your eye on the horses. That's the only reason they'd circle back."

"But the Pawnee's our friends," I say.

"Aye, they are," Beck says. "Until they're not anymore. Go on to your watch, then get some shut-eye."

By the time I fall into my bedroll, sleep is taunting me, and I close my eyes tight against my dreams. Omer is still awake.

"Prometheus?" Omer whispers out into the dark.

"Yeah?"

"You think them Pawnee started the stampede?"

"Don't know," I say. "Too tired to know."

"Prometheus?"

"Yeah?"

"You think Good Eye's done crossed over to heaven?"

"Go to sleep," I say.

"I think he is." Omer is quiet for a time. "You can't take the blame, Prometheus. Ole Woman says it was just an accident. You's lucky you didn't get killed."

I turn my back, stare out at the North Star, and imagine Good Eye's spirit racing the crossroads of heaven. But it don't ease my emptiness.

"I ain't lucky, Omer," I say. "I done tested my fate, and Good Eye paid for it. He weren't no cow horse; I knew that. ..."

"But you didn't—"

"I didn't take care. And I ain't taking care of you either. I dragged you out here away from Daddy Shine. There ain't no mansion and no silver dishes. There ain't no luck. ..." I can't finish. My words lock tight in my throat, and I turn my back against the stars.

CHAPTER TEN

We reach Ogallala.

We wait another day for the sun to do its work while we dope the herd's stampede wounds with thick salve to ward off screwworms.

The next morning, we count out the head, then find a firm spot of ground and cross over the South Platte not a mile west of Ogallala. The water ain't deep, and the beeves make the crossing easy. We camp a safe distance from the rail line and let the animals graze on a spread of sweet grass.

I'm still grieving for Good Eye, but I take up with the sorrel. She's green but minds my lead well enough.

All's quiet from the Pawnee.

This morning brings black-dirt coffee, nothing but grounds boiled over from yesterday, so Beck quits us after breakfast to head to town, cash a money draft, and set up credit at the general outfit store. He barks out orders for watch, promises pay when he gets back, then hollers to get Nack hitched up and over to the town surgeon.

"Boss Beck says that once I get Nack settled in town,

I get the day off," Omer says. "You going into town, Prometheus?" Omer pours out a hot stream of feeble coffee into Rio's tin.

"Not planning on it," I say. Omer's been laboring to raise my spirits, but I been too out of sorts over Good Eye to be much company.

Rio frowns. "Amigo, too much work and no play will make you a dull boy. There are many diversions in Ogallala." Rio grins, then sips his coffee, and steam lingers up around his face. "Come with me to the postmaster to send out my letter. Then, I will show you the town." Rio looks over at me and waits for my answer.

Omer don't wait. "Prometheus, you listen now. You need some cheering up. A little town might be good for you."

"Guess you need help getting Nack to the doctor's," I say. "I'll go."

It takes us more than one attempt to load Nack up into the wagon. His foot is done colored black, and Ole Woman swears the surgeon doctor in Ogallala will saw it off, but Nack won't hear of it.

"Ain't no doctor cutting on me," he says. "Not after the way they butchered up soldier boys during the war." Nack punches out at me with his fists. "You done this to me! You could have saved that boot! I'd be walking now ... you ...!" Nack spews out a line of cuss words, then passes out in a fit of pain and whiskey.

"Pay no mind," Ole Woman says. "It's the pain and the liquor talking."

Beck gets back in time to hand us a half-month's wages and some freedom. "Leave the wagon at the supply store, lads," he says. "They'll load it for us, and I'll get Ole Woman to fetch it home. Beware—word around town is they've got Indian marauders along the Platte. The Bosler brothers' foreman was scalped not three days' ride from here, outside Sidney. They took his clothes, his horse, and his revolver and left bank notes blowing across the plains."

"I bet it was them Sioux devils," Omer says without thinking.

"Don't go looking for trouble, Mr. Shine," Beck warns. "The man should have taken precautions. His poor judgment is not our concern nor our business, rest his soul. Just bewares, and by God's grace, get back to stand your watch." Beck tips his hat at us. "Home by ten, lads."

Omer drives the mules and looks for smooth ground, but for Nack, every bump jars his foot or his sleep, and he starts off on another cussing fit. His foot will be gone before nightfall if the surgeon man's any good.

We cross a little rise, and Ogallala is laid out before us, a dirt street with a handful of windworn buildings facing north toward a line of railroad. Drover's, the general outfitter, is nearest to us, along with the Crystal Palace saloon, the Union Pacific section house, and a jail. A large cattle pen sits at one end of town, with a sea of Texas longhorns ready for shipment to points east. The town is crawling with cowboys and soldiers, hard-looking dance-hall women, drunks, and a few townsfolk.

The doctor works in the tight quarters of a framed, patched sideboard house located halfway down the row, but it's clean, with the sharp odor of medicines and potions. He unwraps Nack's foot, and the swollen, cracked skin oozes a greenish puss. The stench of rotten flesh stings my eyes.

The surgeon pours out a tall glass of whiskey, then downs it in one straight shot. "Foot's got to come off," he says.

We strap Nack down to the kitchen table amidst wild punches and curses while the doctor sucks a clear liquid into a glass tube. "Morphine will make him sleep," he says.

The morphine fills the kitchen with a sweet smell. A sharp-toothed hacksaw lies on a towel, next to a line of butcher knives and needles.

"Hold his leg, boys," the doctor says.

Nack screams out, and before long, the hacksaw gnaws against the bone. The smell of blood and pus and morphine mix in my nose, and a queasy feeling rushes up from my stomach. I race out of the house before I end up sick all over the floor. Before long, Rio and Omer follow.

"You look a little pale, my friend." Rio grins at his own joke.

"I ain't good around surgeon's saws is all," I say.

Rio pulls his flask out of his boot and offers it up to me, but I shake my head. "To Nack," he says, "the brave vaquero who lost his boot and then his foot, but not his life. *¡Salud!*" Rio slams back a full swallow from the flask.

Omer climbs into the wagon. "Shoots, I bet Nack gets one of them peg legs and becomes famous. Probably get one of those nicknames, Peg-Leg Pony Man or something, and ends up in one of them Wild West shows we seen advertised in Dodge City. You remember that, Prometheus? Why, I'd like to see one of them shows before I die."

I know Omer's supposing is just to cheer me up, and I smile over at him best I can, but by the time we drive the wagon to the outfitter store, a dark cloud has taken back my mood.

According to its sign, Drover's is well stocked with groceries, dry goods, provisions, cigars, and liquors, but I ain't called to look through the shelves. Outside the store, a group of white soldiers and cowhands stand around talking about the Indian marauders. From what I can overhear, it's mostly about tracking them Indians down like dogs and murdering every last one of them. Sounds like big talk when the men's all safe on the porch.

Omer buys a sack of taffy and some Bull Durham tobacco to give Nack. "He'll want his smokes when he wakes up," Omer says. "He liked that quirt I made for him. Thinking Boss Beck might let me try a little cowboying, now that Nack done hurt hisself, and Nack might put in a good word for me."

Rio pays six bits for some cigars and a pint bottle of J. F. Cutter whiskey, shipped in all the way from California.

The postmaster ain't nothing but the outfitter clerk wearing a different hat, but Rio hands over his letter and pays for the mailing. By the time we make Deadwood, Rio might hear back from his wife, and I might know how to find *Douglas C. Irwin, Negro speculator.* I put in a few words with the Almighty to send the letter along safe and sure.

"Let me buy you a toddy at the Crystal Palace," Rio says as we leave Drover's.

"I ain't a drinking man," says Omer. "Except once when I slipped a taste of Colonel Dill's elderberry wine. Wheeyee, it was sweet, but it done stung my throat, too."

"Then you can watch me have a whiskey," Rio says. "Come along."

"Think Nack will do good?" Omer asks.

"He will sleep until morning," Rio says. "Morphine is a fine thing when a butcher knife is involved, no?"

There's a hubbub in front of the jail, but the mob is now three men deep, and we can't see the particulars. It's only when we get to the edge of the crowd that we see him. It's the young Pawnee in the army-issue shirt. The one who saved my life. Only he's got a bruised-over eye and a broke nose. Thick chains shackle his feet and hands.

"Let us avoid this trouble," Rio says quietly.

But I work my way up close to the center of the crowd. The Pawnee's dark eyes stare into me, and Mama's breath rallies in my ear. *Take care.* I ain't walking away.

CHAPTER ELEVEN

The Pawnee works some magic.

"Put that heathen in jail and throw away the key!" a man shouts to the angry swarm of soldiers holding fast to the Pawnee.

"Hellfire, string him up now! Let him be an example to them hostiles."

"Or shoot him! That's better treatment than he gave the Boslers' man!"

I talk quiet to the soldier holding the Pawnee. "I hear that foreman got killed three days' ride from here, Sergeant," I say. "This Pawnee was scouting for us then."

"And who are you?" the soldier asks.

"I'm the wrangler with the Diamond Dot outfit—Seamus Beck's the foreman. We're camped just west of town. This Pawnee was with us on the South Platte three days ago."

The soldier sucks his teeth and offers up a snide kind of smile. "You're a Negro, boy. You telling the truth?"

"Ask Beck. Ask any man in our outfit," I say.

"We might get around to that, but this Indian had the

foreman's gun in his possession, and he ain't exactly explaining himself. Makes him look mighty guilty in my book."

I question the Pawnee with my glance. He signs gestures to Rio, and the chains clang against each other.

"Says he traded a white man for it," Rio says.

"Like snow in Hades he did!" The soldier snorts into the air.

"I don't know about the gun," I say, "but he was scouting with our outfit day before yesterday. He couldn't have killed the foreman."

The soldier's eyes steel over to hatred. "I fought for the Union, boy, but don't think I hold any benevolence toward your kind. Now, get on out of here, and let the crowd take care of business."

"The Pawnee didn't—"

But the soldier won't hear no truth. "He's killed plenty," he says. "If not the Boslers' man, then some other sorry whites. It don't matter to me."

"Let the Indian go," I say.

The soldier lays his hand on his gun.

"Easy! *Señores*, easy!" Rio raises his whiskey bottle into the air. "Put your weapons away! All this talk, talk, talk makes my head ache with worry!"

Rio swigs a full gulp of whiskey and sloshes the Cutter down his chin and shirt. He slaps his arm around Omer and swings the whiskey bottle to his mouth, but he misses, and the whiskey pours over his face and hands into the dirt. It splatters on the sergeant's boots. Rio speaks loud and slow. "Your boots, amigo … I didn't … now, now, now, perhaps my friend is mistaken."

Rio staggers over toward me, then leans in close to the soldier and makes a circular motion at his own temple. "The thoughts run free, do they not?" Rio nods, then belches loud not far from the soldier's face.

The crowd laughs, but for a second, it seems as if the soldier might think to shoot Rio. Finally he jerks the bottle away from Rio and throws it in the street.

"Get your colored friends and get out of here," the soldier says.

Rio stumbles to Omer, and his glance tells me to get out of the crowd. I look at the Pawnee, and our eyes lock on each other for a moment. He's a dead man if we don't get him free.

Rio pushes me to the other side of the street. "Come along, Prometheus Jones," he says in a quiet voice. "You cannot sway the good opinions of these fine men without someone dying. I do not wish that to be you, *compadre.*"

"But what will they do to the Pawnee?" I ask.

"If we are lucky, they will put him in jail," Rio says.

"He never killed no foreman," I say. "And I ain't leaving town with him in this fix."

"I understand, but a strong will needs a cool head," Rio says. "Let us go have a whiskey and think."

We walk down the street to the Crystal Palace, and every table in the saloon is full of monte card games and cowboys. Two dancehall girls holler over at Rio and he flirts with them in Spanish, then orders a double-shot whiskey for himself. Omer grins over at the colored barkeep tending a plain plank of wood and orders lemonade.

"No lemonade," the barkeep says. "We got whiskey. You old enough to drink whiskey?"

"I'm eleven," Omer says.

"Then we got milk," the barkeep says. "So it's milk, or milk. Take your pick." Omer orders. I don't want nothing.

"The Pawnee's trouble," Omer says. "They started the stampede, and you can't be sure they didn't kill nobody neither. That Indian had the foreman's gun."

"Omer speaks truth," Rio says. "You can't be certain."

"I am certain," I say. "The Pawnee might have started the stampede. You can't blame them if they knew our cattle was headed to the Sioux. But ride all the way to Sidney and kill a man? Ain't possible."

Rio's whiskey shows up with one of the dancehall girls.

"Two bits," she says. With all the paint on her face, she looks older than Rio, but she's still pretty, with bright red hair and a set of wide blue eyes. Rio pays for the drink and speaks soft in Spanish.

The girl smiles at me. "He's teaching me some Mexican words." She sits down on Rio's lap.

"I'm heading back over to the jail," I say.

"Do not be in such a hurry, amigo," Rio says. "Perhaps a little rest and relaxation will shed light on his guilt or innocence, no?"

"I got just the thing!" Omer drinks his milk down in a shot. "Ole Woman said we can get a bath and a hot supper at the hotel kitchen. And they even got a telegraph office at the railroad house. We could wander downs there directly—send a telegram to Daddy Shine and tell him all our news."

I don't answer.

"Or we could watch them play monte. ..." Omer's voice trails off. "I ain't never seen that game. And I sure would like to wire Daddy Shine before we get out of town."

Rio swallows his drink, then holds up his glass for another and pushes the girl out of his lap. He leans in closer. "You cannot bring this Pawnee's difficulties back to camp. I told you Beck is a patient man, but you do not want to anger him."

The girl brings another whiskey. She smiles at Rio, and he warms up to her like he ain't no married man.

I sit and watch the room. Omer stares over at a card game.

Beck will cut me and Omer loose if I stir up trouble for the herd. We'll never make it to Texas. It won't matter if Irwin is living right in the middle of Lavaca County, with Mr. Jones down the road.

"I'm riding," I say. Omer starts to follow, but Rio nods to let me go alone.

"Ah, you want to be a hero, then, Prometheus Jones?" Rio calls after me. "Is that what you wish?"

"It ain't right is all."

But I don't go to the jail first thing. I ride over to the surgeon and sit with Nack for a spell. He's sleeping with a stub for a foot, but his color is good, and he's got a peaceful air about him. Surgeon says Nack won't be awake until the morning and won't be working the horses no more. I can't do nothing for Nack now.

Out past the jail, the mob is done gone back to Drover's. The Pawnee is nowhere in sight. The sergeant sits out front with a shot glass from the saloon and a cowhide flask. I lift my hat to him respectful like. He don't need to suspect my aim. He raises his glass to me but with a smirk of a smile that lets me know it ain't out of courtesy.

I wander down the street, then take a turn behind the row of buildings and head halfway back. Three small, square windows sit high on the rock walls of the jail. There's no bars, but no man could crawl through the windows either. They're no more than the size of a small patch of quilt. I ride by each window and blow a low whistle out of my throat, but there's no response. I whistle again. Nothing.

I'm set to leave when the sound of chains clang from the first opening. I peer in the dark of the cell and see the Pawnee standing tall in the shadowed light. He's got a fierce kind of look on his face, but he looks small in the cold stone of the room.

"You speak English?" I ask.

"*Irushka*!" he says and slaps his chest with a clank of chain.

"Where's your brother?" I turn and look back out into the flat. The wind blows along the tops of the switch grass until there's nothing but land and sky, but I can't help but feel the other Pawnee is watching us from somewhere.

"I'll be back," I say.

I ride down behind the buildings to the end of town and loop back to Drover's and use my money for a bottle of J. F. Cutter whiskey and some fancy jerky. Then I head back to the Crystal Palace.

Omer's got his eye on the same card game, but Rio has joined the hand. The girl hovers over his shoulder like a pretty vulture.

"He playing?" I ask.

"Playing, but he ain't won yet," Omer says. "I thought you was headed back to camp."

"Rio!" I yell. "Time to go!"

"No, no, no, no, no, my friend." Rio's words run together.

"Leave this boy alone," one of the card players says. "Can't you see he wants to give us all his money?"

"We got to get on back to camp. Finish your bet, but Beck's looking for us." I hate lying to Rio, but the truth won't serve no purpose.

"Have you seen Beck in town?" Rio asks.

"Wagon still over the outfitter's. Figure he's there."

"*Un minuto,*" Rio says. He taps on the table and places a dollar in front of the dealer.

"Don't hurry out, honey. We're just starting to have a

good time," the saloon girl says. She leans in to kiss Rio on the cheek, but he pushes her back from the cards. The dealer shows the winning card, and Rio leans back in his chair.

"Another hand?" the dealer asks.

"We got to go," I say.

"Besides, Lady Luck done give up on you," Omer says. "You done lost three in a row."

"*¡Ya vengo!* I'm coming!" Rio stumbles from his chair and puts on his hat.

The saloon girl pouts up all pretty, and she cuddles herself up against Rio like she might change his mind.

"Have you given up being a hero, Prometheus Jones?" Rio yawns. The girl follows us to the door, tugging on Rio's hand. He ignores her and speaks to me. "Or will you worry me to an early grave? Is it a curse to have a little fun?"

"We got work."

The girl frowns.

"Sorry, miss." Omer tips his hat to the girl like she's some Southern prize.

The girl pulls Rio to her and tries to kiss him, but he says something in Spanish she don't like. She slaps his face hard.

"Come on!" I pull Rio out into the street.

We ride back toward camp.

"Beck is at the outfitter's, you say?" Rio's eyes narrow in the light of the afternoon sun.

"I didn't say that." I circle the horses around, and we end up a half mile behind the row of buildings.

"I thought you talked to him. ..." Rio stops his horse and stares at me.

"I never said for sure."

Rio waits.

"They're holding the Pawnee in jail," I fess up. "I talked to him. Came and got you 'cause I need your help. I can't let that Indian hang. I don't expect Beck will understand. ..."

"Don't expect *I* understand," Rio says. He speaks to me in a low voice. "Who is this Pawnee to you?"

"I can't say exactly."

"I do not like your mysteries, Prometheus Jones. First Irwin, now the Indian. What—"

"Can't say 'cause I don't know! But he saved me," I shouted. "The buffalo would have run me down in that stampede, but the Pawnee grabbed me up. He saved my life, and I can't just leave. ..."

"He saved you?" Omer asks.

I push my boots into my stirrups and look across the flat. "There ain't no right in the world if I let him hang."

Rio squints against the sun. He looks at me like he's considering things. "Do you have a plan?"

"The soldier's drinking whiskey outside the jail," I say. "Figure if you could drink with him some, he might get friendly. Might even fall asleep. Then, I could sneak inside and somehow get the Pawnee out. I ain't figured out the inside part just yet." I pulled the bottle of Cutter out of my saddlebag. "But I wouldn't ask you to drink any old rotgut," I say. "I got some provisions."

Rio sees the bottle and laughs out wide and loud. "Suddenly, I do not hate your idea so much, amigo," he says. He holds up the bottle to show Omer, then hugs it up to himself.

"But that soldier don't like you none," Omer says. "What if you show up and he throws you in jail?"

"A drinking man never turns down good whiskey." Rio smiles, but his face suddenly turns somber. "Wait until the sun is just over the grass," he says. "There is no hurry; the dark will serve you well. But get back to camp. I will not lie to Beck for you if you miss watch." He takes the whiskey and rides back toward Ogallala. "*¡Buena suerte!* You do not know how lucky you are, Prometheus Jones!"

Omer watches as I step out of my saddle, hunt through my saddlebag, and tear off a piece of jerky. "Them people say that Pawnee's guilty," he says. "But you talked to him?"

"He couldn't have rode all the way to Sidney after the stampede. Not even a racehorse could run that hard."

"So you going to help him 'cause he saved your life?"

"I got to," I say. "Do nothing, it's same as if I hanged him myself."

Omer nods but don't speak for a minute. "Prometheus?"

"Yeah?"

"I think them people will hang you, too, if they catch you trying to free that Indian."

"I think you're right."

"And you still want to save him?"

"Yeah."

"You're brave, Prometheus," he says. Omer is quiet for a long minute. "I guess I'm in with you, too. You're my blood kin. Ain't no choice." Omer wipes the sweat from his face with his kerchief. A sheer kind of grit shows up around his eyes.

"Mighty grateful," I say. "Omer?"

He looks at me.

"You're the good cousin."

Omer grins. "I know," he says. "Now, you going to share that jerky or sit there and eat it in front of me?"

I tear off a piece of the jerky. For the first time since Good Eye's broke leg, my gloom melts, and we sit there watching a fine cherry sunset.

Just as the sun falls into the flat, I hike toward the jail. Omer stays back with our horses. I walk around the side of the building and see Rio and the soldier. The stone walls are cool in the shade, and the street is almost empty, except for a crowd of folks mingling around the Ogallala Hotel at the far end of the street. Piano playing drifts down from the saloon.

The soldier tells some loud story, and both he and Rio laugh out full-bellied. I check a side casement, but it's locked. I poke my head around the wall again, and this time Rio's talking. I catch his eye, and he nods toward the other side of the jail, so I make my way around the building. A window is up, and I step inside neat as a whistle.

It's an office of sorts, with an old worn desk on a little

platform and some chairs facing toward it. There's a little pegboard with a circle of keys. I hold them tight in my fingers.

Along the back hall, there are three small cells, stone rooms with big wooden doors cut with tiny windows. The doors to the other cells stand open, but the Pawnee's cell is locked strong and sure. I look at all the keys but don't see one big enough for the lock. All I have is the keys to the shackles.

I whistle low through the window in the door. The Pawnee peers out the window, but neither one of us speaks. He holds his hands out the opening, and I unlock the chain on his wrists. Then he takes the key to do likewise to his feet.

I take a closer look at the cell door, but the lock is too heavy to break. There's no way to get the door open. Rio's voice echoes through the window, and I hear the scrape of chairs on the wooden walk.

"Give me the keys!" I whisper, but there's no answer. The voices are louder now. "Hurry! I need the keys!" I peer into the shadow of the cell, but all I can see is the dull metal of the Pawnee's shackles. It must be some kind of voodoo magic, but the Pawnee is gone!

CHAPTER TWELVE

Soldiers hunt for Rio.

The sergeant's boots land heavy on the stone floor as he opens the door to the building. "Can't be fraternizing at the hotel," he says to Rio. "Have me a prisoner here. But I appreciate the hospitality." His voice is thick with whiskey.

I hear the clang of tin dishes and voices—not just Rio's and the sergeant's.

"Set it down here, boy. Smells too good to give an Indian," the sergeant says. "This will be that Pawnee's last supper if the townspeople got any sense."

Rio talks some more, but I don't listen to his words. My mind is racing to find some place to hide. If the sergeant comes around that corner, he'll find me here.

"Good evening, then," the sergeant says. Rio mumbles something and then the door closes.

There's no escape! I'm caught in the narrow span of hallway in full view—no trace of shade or shadow. The sergeant's breath is just beyond the width of wall. He'll see me for sure once he crosses that doorway. Ain't no place to hide except in one of the open cells, and a shudder jumps through my bones. Once I'm in that four-by-four room, am I a prisoner, too?

But there's no choice. I step into the shadow of the far cell door just as I hear the jingling of his keys. I hug the stone and don't breathe. The keys rattle in the lock.

"Come on now, come on," the sergeant says under his breath, then he speaks to the Pawnee loud. "I ain't letting you out of those shackles, but I'll get the door open in a minute here. Got some grub." The keys jingle more. The door creaks open.

"What the ... Good God and little fishes!" the sergeant yells. But before the words are good out of his mouth, I hear a thump, keys falling to the floor, the clatter of tin dishes, a full sigh of air, and the dull thud of skull against stone. I peer through the slats of the door just as the Pawnee runs down the hallway and out the door. Ain't no voodoo magic. Once his chains were off, that Indian waited to ambush the sergeant.

Behind the jail is the sound of horses' hooves. I jump up to the small slip of the outside window and take in the fading night. The other Pawnee rides full force up to the jail; the freed Indian jumps on a lean mustang, and they disappear into the switch grass.

The sergeant is sprawled out on the stone floor. I can't hear his breathing for the sheer noise of my own, but he smells like a whiskey barrel. He ain't dead—just cold-cocked. There ain't no smirk on his face now.

I hop over his belly and pick up the keys to the shackles, then go back over my paces to the front office, close the open door, and hang up the shackle keys on the pegboard. I step out the window and look around for Rio. He's nowhere in sight. By the time my boots hit dirt, I'm running to find Omer.

"Did you see that?" Omer tosses me the reins of the sorrel. "That Pawnee done run out of there, with the other one waiting on him in the brush."

"Them Pawnee is smarter than both of us," I say. "The sergeant is out cold. Let's go find Rio and get out of here."

"He's not with you?"

"I never saw him once the Pawnee escaped."

"Think he's gone to the Crystal Palace again? We can't go gets him now."

"We ain't got a choice," I say.

We loop around and head toward the end of the street, but we don't get that far. Rio is weaving out of Drover's with a silly grin on his face and a package wrapped in brown paper under his arm.

"Ah, I see you are finished with your business," Rio says. "And since you have come looking for me, I can hope all is well?" Rio's words come out sideways, and he sways back a little as he unties his saddlebag. He ain't faking drunk now.

"That sergeant's going to have a headache, I imagine. Probably don't want to be around town when he wakes up," I say. "The Pawnee got clean away."

"I have bought some ribbon for my wife," Rio says. "Let me give you a piece of advice." He points his finger in the air to call attention to his words. "A man should always be good to his wife." He pats his saddlebag, then looks around like he don't know what to do next.

"Be happy to remind you of that later," I say. "But we need to be heading out."

He wavers as he pulls himself up on his horse and wipes his hand across his mouth to cover a wide yawn. Then a bright air shows in his eyes. "Perhaps we should have a small toddy to carry us back to camp, no?"

I look back toward the jail, and Omer's shaking his head. "I ain't thirsty," he says.

"Best be out of sight," I say. "Come on, Rio, let's go."

Rio don't put up a fuss, so we head back west to the trail and our camp home.

The night turns black with a new moon, but my disposition turns cheerful. Rio snores irregular in his saddle, and Omer prattles on about Nack and Deadwood and Daddy Shine. It pains me Omer didn't get to send a telegram from Ogallala, but we'll have better news from Dakota Territory.

Just outside camp, we catch up with Ole Woman and the wagon. Omer and me help him unload and change about provisions in the chuck box: flour, soda, sugar, salt, baking powder, coffee, beans, and bacon. Rio takes to his bedroll. He'll have some sleeping to do before watch.

"What did you boys think of town? Sight for sore eyes,

ain't it?" Ole Woman talks through his teeth and a new, fat cigar. "I'm surprised you're back here so early."

"Ran out of interest," I say.

"Did you see Nack?" Omer asks as we unload sacks of flour and coffee.

"Still loopy from the morphine," Ole Woman says. "Beck's going over to check on him in the morning before we head out."

"He's ain't going with us?" Omer asks

"Trail's no place for a one-foot cowboy," Ole Woman says, "especially an old cuss like Nack. We'll pick him up on the way south, after we deliver the herd."

"But I done got some tobacco for him at the outfitter's," Omer says.

"Give it over to Beck when he gets here, and he'll take it to him."

"Beck coming in soon?" I ask.

"He said not an hour behind me. Having supper at the hotel with another outfit foreman out of Cheyenne." Ole Woman looks at me. "You boys get some grub in town?"

"Never did," I say.

"I'll get some corned tomatoes going here in a minute. Butchered a calf this morning, if y'all a mind for some blanket steak. Not many of the boys will be in from town, so we can have us a little house party."

Omer follows me as I head over to check on the remuda. The horses are tethered loose along a line of heathered grass near the camp.

"Prometheus, I want to be your helper now that Nack's took to his bed," Omer says. "But I can't talk to Boss Beck, so you gotta talk to him."

"What do you want me to say?" I ask.

"That you needs help," Omer says. "That you needs *my* help."

"You willing to ride a horse all day and pull night watch half the night?"

Omer's got a hopeful look about his face. "I figure if I'm a cowboy, Boss Beck won't fret about keeping me on. I'll work hard."

"Ole Woman works you hard. I seen him," I say. "And you'll get the hang of camp cooking if you want. Your stew weren't that bad. Besides, there's not a cowboy in camp that's better at working leather—an outfit needs good rigging. Beck would be the first to swear to that."

"But Boss Beck don't give any count to pot rustling and braided rawhide," Omer says. "I want me a man's job."

I look at Omer. He's growed an inch since we left the home place; now he's nearer a man than a boy. I can't be always thinking of him as just a kid. "Okay," I say. "But I can't promise that Beck will be willing. I ain't exactly in his good graces either."

Omer's eyes light up the earth. "Wheeyee! You won't be sorry, Prometheus! I promise, cross my heart and hope to die."

"Start by helping me unsaddle our horses, then rein in the remuda closer to the wagon," I say. "I don't want the horses sheared out like this for the night."

Omer and I get to work, and before long Ole Woman is calling for supper. Beck's still in town, and ain't nobody in camp except the cowboys on watch, a sleeping Rio, and us, so we eat our grub together. Omer wants to tell Ole Woman about his plans, and I got to figure out a way to get Beck's say-so.

I wash the sweat off my face and get ready to eat. My paper with Mama's words still sits tight inside my hat, and I got a restless feeling all the sudden to get back on the trail.

"Omer told me about your family," Ole Woman says to me. "Your ma died?"

"From consumption. Last year," I answer.

"Where's your pappy?"

"Ain't never knowed my daddy," I say. "You been working for Beck a long time?"

"Coming up a year." Ole Woman sops up the gravy from his steak with a biscuit. "He's real set on getting his business done. Beck ain't always nice, but he's fair with folks if they do their job. Pays on time when the herd's delivered. He don't get too personal with any of the boys, but I've worked for less men."

Omer looks over at me through the fire. "What do you think he's gonna do about Nack?" Omer asks.

"Nothing," Ole Woman says. "Don't expect another hand will want to hire on now that we're almost on Sioux territory."

"Think he'll let me do some cowboying?" Omer asks.

Ole Woman stops chewing. “You anxious to give up working the wagon?”

“It’s just ... I can’t ...” Omer’s lip starts shaking. “I don’t think … I never learned …”

“You can’t cook?” Ole Woman looks full serious for a minute, then grins up a yellow-toothed smile. “You like eating more than cooking. Is that right?”

Omer’s mouth turns a little sideways.

“Be plenty of work for all of us until we get to Deadwood,” Ole Woman says. “Imagine you can get in some herding. Go on and ask Beck. I ain’t got no quarrel with it.” Ole Woman holds his cigar stub to the coals of the fire, then holds it to his lips and sucks in his lungs. The stub glows a pure red.

“Thought Omer could help with the wrangling some,” I say. “Could use a hand.”

We finish up the steak and sit and watch the glow of Ole Woman’s cigar. I’m nodded off when we hear some horses ride in. Figure it’s Beck, but when I open my eyes, a half-dozen United States Army soldiers is talking to Big Henry out on watch. I feel for the handle of my Colt, and Ole Woman, me, and Omer get up to take a look. Within a minute, the soldiers are staring down at us.

“Got a Mexican here named Rio?” one of the soldiers asks. “I got orders to bring him in.”

CHAPTER THIRTEEN

Beck's temper shows itself.

Ole Woman rubs his cigar on the heel of his boot. "What's the trouble? We got a cowboy named Rio, but he's passed out drunk to the world."

"Not my job to answer questions, old man," the soldier says. "We're just here to bring him in."

I offer up some conversation to give me time to think. "We met up with Rio at Drover's, and he rode out here with us," I say. "Don't mean to keep you from your business, sir, but he in trouble?" Omer and I trade glances.

The soldier talks out in a tight voice. "A murdering Pawnee escaped jail this evening. The captain wants to ask your friend some questions. Now where is he?"

Ole Woman don't let on if he's scared of them soldiers. "We had Pawnee scouts with us three days ago. They worked for the outfit all the way from Kansas. Never caused no trouble, no sir. Not a peep from them boys. One of them get—"

The soldier interrupts. "*Where* is the Mexican?" He ain't making no social call.

"We can get Rio to ride into town in the morning," Ole Woman says. "Heap easier than trying to get him up and about tonight."

"I've got orders," the solider says. His voice is as sharp as an overseer's. "We'll take him in tonight. He can talk all he wants with the captain tomorrow."

"Don't much matter one way or t'other. But I sure wouldn't want to haul that cowboy's carcass into town if I was you. Worse than a two-hundred-pound tow sack. You probably hear him snoring if you'd a mind to listen." Ole Woman wipes out his skillet and turns to wash up our soaking dishes. "He's sacked out behind the wagon yonder." Ole Woman talks slow and puts on a show for them soldiers, but he signals me, and I catch a shadow behind the remuda. The horses stir up some.

"Guess I better saddle my mount. Watch coming up," I say loud enough for the soldiers to hear. I don't wait for them to walk behind the wagon. Omer follows me.

"Saddle Rio's night horse," I whisper. "If the soldiers ask, you got watch, too."

Omer flies a blanket over the horse's back. "Where's Rio?" He mouths out the words without no voice.

But his question is answered by the shouts of the soldiers.

"He can't be far!" one of them yells.

"Hurry up!"

"Search the wagon."

The soldiers tear into the bed and chuck box, and

within a minute every cowboy's roll is torn apart, with pots and pans and supplies thrown upside down and tumbled into the grass.

"I don't know what makes you think a man can hide in a flour sack," Ole Woman yells. "Ain't nothing in there's any of your doing."

"Are you harboring this man? I'll take you in, too, if you start sassing me." The soldier shouts orders to his men. "Search the grass! Shoot the Mexican if you have to, but don't kill him!"

"You get all trigger-happy, we might get us a stampede, now," Ole Woman says. "Can't be stirring up a stampede, I tell you. You ever see a man stomped bloody into the dirt?"

"Out of our way!" the soldier yells.

The cows are beginning to stir now. Some of the beeves are standing up, and the horses at the back of the remuda are moving restless and worried.

Just as we get Rio's horse saddled, Beck and one of the cowhands from watch ride into camp.

"Holy Mother in heaven, what are you doing?" Beck shouts at the soldiers. He pulls up his horse and almost jumps from his saddle.

"We've got orders to take in the Mexican from this outfit, and we're taking him in." The soldier waves his quirt in the air.

"If you stampede this herd, man, I'll throw you to the steers myself," Beck shouts. "Now, call off your men!"

Omer nods and holds watch while I quiet-like walk Rio's mount to the back of the remuda, humming low in my throat to ease the horses' jitters. I don't wait for Rio to show himself; I leave the horse with its reins dangling in the dirt. The animal won't have to wait long. I head back and saddle my own night horse.

The soldiers and Beck are more civil now, but there ain't no love lost between them.

"We want the man Rio for questioning." The soldier's voice is flat but solid. He ain't leaving without Rio if he can help it.

"Questioning for what, eh?" Beck pulls at his mustache with his thumb and forefinger. Frustration gathers in his eyes.

"A Pawnee was responsible for the cold-blooded murder of the Bosler brothers' foreman. Seems he might have been working for you ..."

"A Pawnee scout working for me, now?" Beck throws back his head and laughs out full and long. "You arrested our Pawnee scout? Which one? Do you even know there are two?" Beck laughs again, but this time his laughter is bitter and mocking. "Half the Sioux nation wants to kill every white between here and Deadwood, and you've arrested a Pawnee scout? Heaven forbid, man, I feel much safer knowing the U.S. Army is protecting us."

"I have my orders—"

"And I have three thousand beeves to deliver to Fort Peck—your witch-hunt for the Pawnee is nothing but a distraction, man. Where's your sense, now? Rio is not in camp, so get out and leave us to our work." Beck waves his hand like a white woman sending off a yard full of children and goes about his business.

The soldier looks at Beck like he don't know what to do. He stands around for a minute, then mounts his horse and shouts orders to the other men.

"We'll search back along the river into Ogallala," he says. "The Mexican can't have gone far."

It don't take a hundred heartbeats until I hear the sound of Rio's horse hightailing it west along the Platte. Beck hears it, too. He looks sharp at me, then watches the soldiers ride along the horizon back toward town.

My bet's on Rio—the soldiers don't seem too keen on hunting much beyond the safety of the rail line.

Omer helps Ole Woman settle things back into the wagon. The cattle is bawling and fidgety. Beck hollers for Big Henry to fill in for Rio, but Omer volunteers up for watch duty, and me and Ole Woman vouch for him until Beck finally nods yes. Big Henry leans back into the wagon wheel with his coffee, content for some grub and some sleep. Beck studies his tea and don't look up.

Out on the flat, Omer passes me twice in the dark, sitting tall and alert. "With Rio gone, Boss Beck might be real happy to see me cowboying."

"I'll talk to him about you," I say. "But I got to take care. Other than getting this herd to Deadwood, I can't figure a lick what Beck's thinking. If he's a mind that I put Rio up to helping me free that Pawnee, he won't be calling me no lucky charm."

"You worried about Rio?"

"Figure he'll show up."

The beeves bellow out into the dark. Tuttle and Con ride into camp from Ogallala.

Omer's shoulder slumps a little. "Think we'll ever end up with that mansion for Daddy Shine, Prometheus? Seems far away ..."

"Can't tell yet," I say. "Something good to dream about, I reckon." I press my heel into the sorrel's side. "Let Beck get some sleep, and I'll judge things in the morning. Ride on now."

But I don't have to wait until morning. The Big Dipper lines up at midnight when Beck rides out to meet me at the far end of the herd's bedding ground.

"All quiet," I say.

Beck don't offer no niceties. "We'll start toward Sidney soon as the grass dries in the morning," he says. "I suspect your Pawnee friends have moved south, eh?"

I don't answer.

"Did you hear me make the speech about staying out of Indian business?" Beck talks quiet, but his eyes are smoldering hot.

Beck don't want no words. I stare back at him.

"Are you hard of hearing, lad?" Beck's voice is harsh, but I can't tell how balled up his anger is.

"Not as I know," I say.

"I couldn't put it together full before. But you and Rio helped that Pawnee escape, didn't you?"

"You said yourself he wasn't guilty."

"And I understand you made a point of informing the sergeant and the townspeople that was your lofty opinion."

"The Pawnee was innocent, that's all. I said as such. How did you—"

"It's my bloody business to know everything about this outfit!" Beck's voice raises up just enough to rile a few cattle. He looks across the horizon, wipes his finger and thumb along his mustache, and breaths out slow. "Did you help the Pawnee escape, sir?" The green in Beck's eyes glows like an evil spirit. He already knows my answer.

"I did," I say. "They wanted to hang him; it weren't right—"

Beck don't let me finish. "And Rio was part of your shenanigans?"

"He was drinking with the sergeant, that's all. Never knew what I had planned," I lie to Beck. Better that he don't blame Rio for my trouble. "I stole the key when the soldier wasn't looking and unlocked the Pawnee's shackles. But the Indian freed hisself when the soldier took in his supper. Nobody saw me. Lucky, I guess."

Beck reaches over and pulls me out of my saddle until his face ain't more than a boot's length in front of me. "Well, what a fine example of righteousness you are, boy!" Beck's voice hisses into my face. "A regular lawman, aren't you now?" Beck pushes me back, and I grab the saddle horn to keep from falling off my horse.

Ain't no anger on Beck's face, but his eyes hold a meanness that ain't no stranger to me. Every white man got some of it.

"I ought to take a whip to you!" he says. "Rio was a good swingman, so now we're headed into Sioux territory without his help or his gun. We're down two men, so I can't afford to let you go, but if you go meddling in affairs that are not your concern and keep me from delivering this herd, I'll leave you on the trail where you stand, and there'll be no looking back."

Beck wheels his horse around next to mine and talks without a bit of feeling in his voice. "We'll see who's lucky then."

A chill in Beck's eyes tells me he's no bluff.

"Hold the herd until Mr. Shine rallies the morning guard," he says. Beck don't even wait for me to say anything, and he's gone.

I squeeze my eyes shut for a minute and pray for Mama's strength. I know I done right by the Pawnee, and I ain't looking back, but now that I been at the hand of Beck's temper, Texas seems as far away as them morning stars.

CHAPTER FOURTEEN

We head west to Sidney.

Come full morning, Beck divides up the chores after breakfast, then heads into town to work out arrangements for Nack to stay with the surgeon. Big Henry and Con take count of the herd, and we wait for dry grass and Beck's return, but an hour don't pass until Beck comes down the trail with Nack sitting behind him, cussing out words I ain't never heard. Nack is pale and glassy-eyed, but not even the doc's morphine can keep him from mouthing off as cranky as ever.

"He's too cantankerous for the good doctor," Beck says. "And I can't wait for an improved disposition and better arrangements. Let him ride with Ole Woman, and Mr. Shine can work drag with you, Prometheus. At least we'll have another iron if there's trouble later on."

"Get me over to the wagon," Nack yells. He slips off Beck's horse, leaning on a rude crutch made from the crook of a tree branch. "I ain't staying with no sawbones!" he says. "Them bloodthirsty scoundrels cut before they look until a man don't have no self-respect left. Every one of them! I can pull my weight good as any man here." Nack looks over at me. "Least I can swim without near drowning a man."

Omer tries to help him up to the spring seat, but Nack pulls away. "I don't need no help, boy," he says, and he hoists himself up in the wagon with the strength of a man whose pride means more than pain. "Get on the trail," he orders Ole Woman.

"I done got you some tobacco for when you was sickly," Omer says. "Boss Beck rode off this morning without it." Omer hands up a small burlap pouch, and Nack considers it until he realizes we're all watching him.

"I ain't taking no presents from you," he says. His face is broke out in a full-sized sweat, but he sits stiff and straight on the wagon. "And I don't oblige your pity."

Ole Woman takes in Omer's disappointment, then shakes his head and slaps the reins on the mules and sets out.

I try to bust the sting of Nack's slight. "Go on and saddle one of them string horses," I say to Omer.

Omer pockets the tobacco and smiles some, but I know he ain't right about it.

"Nack was sour before his leg got cut," I say. "Ain't no changing a man's nature."

When Omer gets seated, we hurry on some lazy beeves and chase the herd west along the piece of pie-shaped land formed by the north and south forks of the Platte River. Beck and Big Henry stay with General Custer and the chuck wagon in the lead. Tuttle and Con ride forward swing, then me and Omer follow.

Our plan is to stay along the rail line right-of-way until we get to Sidney, then turn straight north toward Box Butte through the Black Hills to Deadwood. Beck says the chances of Indian raiders are small between here and our turn north, but we should be careful with double-man guards and a nighthawk for the remuda.

"You thinks Boss Beck likes me now?" Omer says as the cattle stretches out along the trail. "He done promoted me and all."

"He did," I admit. I don't tell Omer about Beck's temper. "Figure we can split up nighthawk watch if you want. I'll let you take first guard, then I'll finish out and get the horses set for morning."

"How long you think it is before we make Deadwood?" Omer asks. "We never did get no telegram to Daddy Shine while we's in Ogallala, and I hate that awful. Think he's pining over us?"

"He knows you're doing all the good," I say. "Don't fret after it. We'll be in Deadwood in another month."

"If the Sioux don't get us?" Omer asks.

"They ain't going to bother us. Beck's too dogged to get the herd through," I say. "Keep close watch and don't lag none, and we'll be all right."

Omer grins up wide. "We got to get us some gold in Deadwood, now. Daddy Shine needs them silver dishes."

The cattle are slow to move off the sweet grass, and Beck

is eager to keep the herd together and things moving. Me and Omer fan our hats and slap our ropes all day, but the cattle linger like they're around a Thanksgiving supper table. And the horses ain't no better.

Beck scouts ahead of the trail, anxious about Indians. He suspects the Sioux knows we're here, but he don't plan for any hostiles while we're so close to the rail. Once, I think I see a rider on the edge of the horizon behind us, but I don't call attention to it. Beck says Indians don't ride alone.

The beeves seem restless toward evening, and it's dark by the time they're settled. We make camp a mile back from a shallow creek and tether the horses to a rope tied from the chuck wagon to a skinny line of scrub brush. Omer takes on watch while I rest my eyes. Ole Woman hovers over Nack and Con playing a game of hearts while I unroll my bed and lay it out on a patch of soft ground, then pull off my boots.

A wolf howls a long yelp from far off in the dark. "You ain't going to hobble them horses?" Nack asks as he flips a card over for Con to see.

"Ain't planned on it," I say.

"You ain't nothing but a tinhorn. A pack of wolves gets in the middle of them animals, you'll be hunting horses sure as you know it."

"The horses ain't left to wandering," I say. "Besides, we got a fire. That should keep the wolves away."

"And you leaving that bottle washer to watch?" Nack is full of questions.

"He's got good eyes and ears."

"He been around horses much?"

"Enough."

"Enough ain't near good enough." Nack's been nudging me all evening about my judgment as wrangler.

"You gonna play cards or talk?" Con asks.

Nack slaps down his card while I fall into my bedroll and turn my back to him.

But he can't leave it alone. "I don't give a whoop if the whole remuda ends up in the same shape as that dead horse of yours."

Nack starts picking on Con, and I fall asleep. I dream about Mama and the Dill boys and Good Eye and Levi. When Omer wakes me for guard, I jump out of my sleep, only it ain't Omer standing over me. It's Rio. I think I'm still dreaming and start to speak out, but he hushes me and makes a motion to meet him out beyond the horses.

I get dressed and tie up my bedroll, then pour two cups of thick coffee into tins. Omer sits nodding with his back to a rock, a half-braided quirt almost slipping out of his hands. The horses are quiet, and the night air is thick with the smell of animals. I set the coffee down, then wake Omer. His eyes tell me he's hurt I done found him sleeping, but I half smile and tell him to go get some real shut-eye. He don't argue.

I wait with my coffee, and in a minute Rio steps out of the shadows.

"*¡Hola!* Prometheus Jones! It seems you have found me."

I shake Rio's hand and pass over some coffee to him. "I wondered if that was you earlier on the horizon."

"One and the same," Rio says. He looks rested and none the worse for hiding on the flat. "How is our Señor Beck?"

"He's got a temper."

"Ah, what did I tell you, my friend?" Rio drinks his coffee and looks out at the sky. "It will be morning soon. I will speak to Beck, but first I must know the details of our story. What did you tell him?"

"That I helped the Pawnee escape."

"You?"

"Didn't mention your part in it, but he's curious, I reckon, with the soldiers looking for you. I guess you got a right to be angry with me."

"What's done is done. The soldiers will not come this far looking for me. So, we have had our adventure, no, Prometheus Jones?" Rio knocks my coffee tin with his.

"I'm grateful," I say. "I'll probably never see that Indian again, but at least I'm back in fate's good graces. Just got to worry about Beck now."

"As for Beck, I will blame my troubles on J. F. Cutter," Rio says. "He won't like it, but I will play on his greed and ignore his temper."

"Beck's worried about the Sioux," I say.

"He is a practical man."

"You see any sign of Indians?"

"No, but the sergeant talked freely. The Sioux chief Crazy Horse will not go easy. There will be trouble." We sit in the dim light and drink our coffee like old friends.

"Nack's come along with us," I say. "Mighty bossy, too—"

"... For a man full of morphine and whiskey?" Rio laughs. "Do not take his words so close to your heart. It is not you who troubles him."

"What eats at him, then?"

Rio shrugs. "His ugly face, perhaps?"

I can't help but laugh.

Rio downs the last of his coffee. "¡Buenas noches!" he says. "I will see you in the daylight."

I let the horses out to graze and water before the sun gets up good. Beck will be happy to see Rio. Reckon my luck ain't done yet.

CHAPTER FIFTEEN

Nack tells a story, and Beck plays a trick.

Beck welcomes Rio back into camp like the prodigal son, but even with an extra set of eyes, it ain't a full sunup and sundown until we lose two beeves while nooning near Water Holes. Tuttle and Con hunt about for the calves, but they're as gone as if their animal spirits done vanished in smoke, sacrificed to some god.

The next morning, two well-heeled prospectors looking for safe passage to Deadwood catch up to us from Sidney. After some brief words, Beck agrees to take them along for the show of guns.

One of the men sports a Texas saddle on a fine stallion, along with a Winchester '73 carbine and a nickel-plated, ivory-handled .45 Colt. He slinks along like a snake charmer, but my thought is he'd smile or shoot you, whatever pleased him. Beck says his name is Cornelius Donahue, and he and his friend are from Philadelphia looking for the gold fields and a year of genuine adventure. It don't hurt none that Donahue been up Buffalo Gap before and knows the country.

The other fella is named Edward Wheeler. He's pale-skinned, with curly black hair and a fancy suit and waistcoat. He keeps a stiff-board notebook in his pocket, always writing notes on the trail, but he's got a fine Cloverleaf revolver, too. Rio and I bet he ain't never got a shot off.

Even though it's good weather, the remuda worries me all afternoon with its skittish behavior; there's company hiding in the buffalo grass, and the horses know it. We set camp on a divide overlooking Greenwood Valley. A mighty tower of earth and stone sits off to our west. Rio calls it Chimney Rock. This is fine territory. Ain't no wonder the Sioux are fighting to hold on to the land.

Omer and I feed and water, then hobble the horses for the night. Grub ain't more than jerked strips of beef and buffalo as Beck don't opt for no campfire.

It's just sundown when we encounter the Sioux for the first time. Drums. Nothing but drums.

The rhythm is distant and steady, so the beeves don't take no offense, but every cowboy in camp is edgy. Omer works a piece of hide, and Rio smokes a fat cigarette. Nack nips whiskey from a hip flask, while Ole Woman passes about a worn paper bag of lemon drops. Beck rides every watch, without an ounce of sleep in him. And all the time, we listen to distant drums like they ain't there. But they is.

"You ever seen a man lose his scalp?" Nack asks Wheeler.

"Can't say that I have, sir," he says. "Must be something horrendous."

"It's a bloody mess." Nack spits out into the grass. "I rode with a west Texas outfit right after the war. One morning a brown speck comes up out of the dust lickety-split, like some God Almighty terror. Ended up being George Henley's horse. He was a puncher riding with us, looking for lost calves, just like today."

"Was he hurt?" Wheeler sits knocking the mud off his boots with a stick of kindling from the chuck wagon.

"No, he was dead." Nack waits for Wheeler's reaction. There ain't none. "George weren't nowhere in sight. But tied onto the saddle horn was a bundle and a note, and if it don't beat it to Betsy, there was a baby girl in that bundle."

"Scalped?"

"No! Alive as I'm sitting here talking to you but cried out from bouncing all over Texas."

Wheeler leans forward and finds his notebook. "What did the note say?" He wets the point of his pencil and huddles up over the paper in the dark.

"Trouble. Her papa shot through the heart by them heathen hostiles. Her mama done dragged off. George's last act on this earth was to write that note and slap the rump of that horse."

The drums pound through the last of Nack's words, and he takes a swallow of whiskey. "Found George's body the next day with six arrows in it, and his head bare. Scalped to the skull. Worst thing I ever seen. Blood everywhere. Burned-out wagon. Even stole the boots off George's feet.

Never knew if he went to sleep without them or if they took his boots off him."

"That's ghastly!" Wheeler cries.

Ole Woman looks over at me. "What happened to the baby?" he asks.

Nack don't answer.

"What *did* happen to the girl?" Wheeler repeats as he scribbles on his paper.

"The boys named her *Sunny* after the baby bonnet she was wearing. Turned her over to a widow woman in town. Never heard no more about her. Never did find them beeves neither."

"But señor, *por favor*, didn't they find the calves hiding in a canyon?" Tobacco flames up in a gray ribbon around Rio's head. "And the girl's name was *Sunshine* the last time you told this story, no? Last year ... on the drive to Wichita?"

Nack's voice cracks hard in the dark. "What in Hades do you know about it? I didn't ask your opinion. You saying I'm a liar?"

"Not at all, my friend. I just have a good memory. It is a curse, I swear."

I can feel myself smiling in the dark.

"Peeeeshawww, were you pulling my leg, old man?" Wheeler asks. "I thought you were telling me a true story!"

"Ever bit of it is true! So what if I done told it before, I ain't no liar."

Wheeler straightens up and puts the notebook back in his pocket. "Sir, I believe a man ought to get his facts straight in his storytelling. Besides, it's peculiar to me that you would want to position a tale like that as truth with those drums playing in your ears. Despite my appearance, I'm not some scared-silly tenderfoot. *I* am a novelist. Good night, gentlemen!"

Nack pulls his crutch over to him and directs his voice over to Rio. "If I had me another foot, I'd put my boot right in the seat of your pants. I ain't no liar."

"But you do not have another foot, my friend. So I will forgive your bad humor."

"I'm going to bed." Nack pushes himself up to the cradle of his crutch.

Rio grins. "Buenas noches. Sleep well."

Big Henry starts to snicker. I bump Omer's shoulder, and he starts grinning, too.

"What's a novelist?" Omer asks.

"A fancy-pants writer, hear him tell," Ole Woman says as he rolls a lemon drop along his teeth.

"Think he'll want to make us famous in one of his stories?" Omer's eyes shine up with excitement.

"Perhaps he will," Rio says. "All save Señor Nack."

Con smirks up a laugh. Them Sioux drums don't seem so wicked now, and several of the boys unroll their beds for the night. But Nack gets the last laugh; ain't a one of us takes off his boots for sleeping.

The next day, we're hoping to make the North Platte

River, but midmorning we see a lone Sioux on the horizon. Beck and Donahue is riding with me, asking about some frayed rigging on Donahue's saddle.

"I can bet he's not riding unaccompanied," Beck says. "Now they know we're here, lads." Beck's body tightens, and Donahue's eyes run cold.

The Sioux rides right for us, and Beck heads out to meet him. Donahue follows. I circle back to hurry on a sore-footed steer, then chase after them. They're less than five rods from the Indian when the glint of gunmetal catches my eye, and I see Donahue pull out his .45 Colt. Beck ain't looking back. Donahue finds his mark. He's set to gun down the Indian!

But I ain't for killing first and talking later. I strike my Colt out of my belt like a hot match, and just as Donahue cocks his pistol, the bullet from my gun blazes across the grass and catapults his iron into the air, leaving Donahue hugging his hand to his side. Still, a wild shot rings out from his gun, and the Indian slumps and falls to the ground. His pony spooks and runs toward Chimney Rock.

The herd veers back from the sound of the shot, but don't stampede. Beck reins his horse around and screams out at Donahue. "Why in God's name did you want to shoot, man? Are you daft? Have you no wits at all about you?"

Donahue shrugs his shoulder. "Now the hostile isn't alive to tell we're here, Mr. Beck. I'm protecting my interests and yours."

"You think they're not going to find out three thousand head of cattle are waltzing through their land?" Beck's face is ruddy with anger. "I'm the one to decide the shooting, I thought I made that clear. ..."

"Good grief, man, it was just an Indian." Donahue seats his Colt in its holster.

Beck motions over to the body. "Mr. Jones, see if he's dead. And get me Mr. Donahue's gun."

The Indian ain't much more than a boy. His face is smooth as the brown glaze pot my mama used to serve wild root tea. "He's a kid," I say. "Looks like the bullet grazed him, but he hit his head on a rock. Must have knocked him out."

"Bring him to camp," Beck says. "Mr. Donahue, all you've done is start up a rile that may get every one of us parted from our scalps. You and Mr. Wheeler are no longer welcome. You can stay until we reach Camp Clarke. After that, you're gone. And I'll keep your gun while you're with us."

Donahue starts to argue, but Beck rides off fast.

The Sioux boy is of a sturdy build, but I haul him up over the sorrel, and his hair dangles down along the animal's flanks. The boy smells of sweet smoke and buffalo meat.

I ride with the body back to the herd. Beck's jaw is popping in and out something fierce. "Take him to Ole Woman to bandage up his wound," he says. "Then bind his hands and feet, and let him ride in the wagon until he wakes up."

"Yes, sir," I say.

"I'm indebted to your steady hand, lad. We'll avoid their fight if we can."

"Yes, sir." I see the thinking in Beck's eyes.

"That pinto in the remuda," he starts.

"But that horse ain't fit for riding. He's a devil, ready to break free and head back to Texas first chance he gets."

"Come find me when we stop midday," Beck says. "Could be that horse will be a godsend."

It's already afternoon when we finally rest the beeves. We soak up our hardtacks in cold coffee. Donahue don't join us, but Mr. Wheeler hangs back to the edge of our conversation.

"I say the only good Indian is a dead Indian," Nack says. "Beck's a fool for turning out Donahue. We'll need good guns once we get over the Platte. Beck's so dang set of staying out of Indian business, he's going to end up right in it."

"I don't like shooting children," Ole Woman says. "Even if they is Indians."

"Indians ain't human!" Nack yells. "Every one of those Sioux brats would slit our throats first chance they got."

"Do you suppose he is serious about setting us out?" Mr. Wheeler asks.

"Beck's a hothead, but he ain't a cruel man." Ole Woman pours round the last of the coffee. "He won't make you leave, Mr. Wheeler. He'll kill you himself before he set you and Donahue off alone in this country."

Con rides up with his spyglass. Just on the horizon, a small band of Sioux sits studying our camp. "We got us some company, boys," he says.

Every hand runs for his mount, but Beck rides into our midst. "Hold up, gentlemen! Let's be smart here," he says. "It's a small party. They're probably looking for the boy."

"He's still out cold," Ole Woman says.

"Then let's give them a little show, lads. Prometheus, get the pinto, and a couple of you men lash the boy to the horse, headed south. Let him take a ride and see if the Sioux follow. Savages or no, this boy needs to be back with his people, and if the pinto does his job, it just might be enough of a distraction to let us get to the river. Ole Woman, get ready to roll!"

"Are you turning Donahue over to them?" Wheeler's hand shakes, but he's got out his notebook and pencil again.

"No, sir, I am not. But if they find out Donahue is responsible and want him, I won't risk my herd. Not for any man's hide. Let's go, gentlemen."

The boy seems more awake, but he's stumbling like a drunk. On his feet, he moves more like a man than a boy. He pulls away from Con, and opens his eyes full when Rio heaves him over his shoulder.

"Forgive my haste," Rio says. "But we do not have time to tarry, my friend."

I nudge the sorrel next to the pinto and hold the horse's head to the side while Rio and Con get the boy straddled on the horse. He's slumped forward and lashed to the pinto's flank and neck with a rope of rawhide.

The boy wakes more, and some gut feeling takes hold of me. If the boy wakes up full, ain't nothing about Beck's plan going to work. A high-strung pinto might be no match at all for an Indian boy's horse sense.

Like a flash of lightning, the boy sits up and his rawhide ropes dig into the pinto's chest. The horse rears up, and the sorrel starts to spook. I press my knees into the sorrel and hold on to the pinto's rein with all my might. Rio grabs for the boy, but the pinto stomps sideways, and Rio jumps to get out of harm's way. The Indian boy jerks his hands around to his side to try to rip the reins from my hands. The pinto shudders, with wide eyes and straight ears. I can't hold the horse any longer.

"Don't mean no harm," I yell to the boy. My balled-up fist connects hard to the boy's jaw just as I let go of the pinto's rein. The horse don't move, then takes off running with the boy flopping cattywompus on the pinto's back until the dirt smokes up behind them for a quarter mile.

Beck is right. Ain't no Sioux party could miss our little show, and they're riding like the wind to catch up to the pinto.

"Bravo!" Mr. Wheeler about sings out the good news. "They're following!" A look of relief passes over his face.

"Let us go the other direction," Rio says as he mounts his horse. "*¡Vamos!* Quickly."

Beck's already with General Custer and a string of

beeves spread out over a wide sward of land, hurrying north.

Mr. Wheeler hangs back and spies the Indian party as it disappears along the ridge. "What a fine picture for a poet's pen!" he says. "Beck is a genius, and you, my boy, are the true grit and gumption of the West!" Wheeler rides off to join Rio.

"What if he writes you up in one of his stories?" Omer asks. "You might get famous!"

Famous? Would Mr. Jones hear about me all the way to Texas?

CHAPTER SIXTEEN

The North Platte betrays us.

It's near dark when we make Camp Clarke, but the place is lined with folks waiting to cross the North Platte. The river is at flood stage, broad and swift-flowing, but there's a brand-new bridge for daylight crossing and a line of five freight wagons and a stagecoach waiting for the sun. Beck holds the herd back a mile from the river, and we make camp.

True to his word, Beck sends Mr. Wheeler and Donahue from our company, but seeing how there's several bands of prospectors and a new-built saloon at the start of the bridge, Donahue don't seem to care much. Mr. Wheeler argues mighty big words with Beck but follows Donahue along like a scorned woman, fussing the whole time. Rio and Big Henry take the first watch. Ole Woman lights up a fire, and we stuff our faces with biscuits, white-flour gravy, beefsteaks, and fried onions.

After supper, Beck talks with Nack, and I strain my ears to hear what they're saying. I know Nack schemes to spoil my good standing with Beck any chance comes along. I got to watch out after myself.

"I'll pay the toll for the wagon, eh, but we'll swim the beeves and horses," Beck says.

"That's near thirty rods of swimming." Nack points toward the water. "You'll have to find a place to hold up halfway so they can rest."

"There's an island not far down the bank." Beck folds a piece of map and squares it straight into his vest pocket.

"Work them in shifts, or they'll crowd each other to the footing. Once we get General Custer across, they'll see the old boy and want to follow him. You'll have to hold them off, and we'll swim—"

"You won't be swimming with the herd," Beck says matter of fact.

"What do you mean?" Anger jumps into Nack's voice.

"You know full well what I mean, man," Beck says. "You're still on morphine. Your limb's not fully healed. I won't risk it . . . not for you. Not for the herd."

"You telling me I can't do it?" Nack's words are fast and harsh and loud enough for the whole outfit to overhear. "Don't need a foot to go swimming! I done saw this herd across every piece of river from here to Texas. I'll do this one, too!"

"No you won't. You'll ride over with the wagon."

"And who in Hades is going to swim General Custer across?"

Beck looks over to me. "Mr. Jones, are you up for a bit of adventure now?"

"That kid half drown me in the Republican! He's the

reason I'm a poke and a step now. He couldn't even reach out and grab a boot floating right in front of him." Nack throws down his plate. "You're a fool if you going to trust him!"

Every cowboy around the fire stops and looks over at Nack.

"You all know it's true! I'm the only hand that can swim this herd across. I don't need a foot to swim that river." Nack looks back at the cowboys staring at him. "Any you boys ready to sign up and swim these beeves over with a tinhorn darky?"

Beck reaches over and grabs Nack's shirt. "You'll want to shut up, sir," he says. "You're testing my patience and my loyalty, and you'll find that to be a mistake. Mr. Jones did a fine job on the Republican. You lost your boots, man, not the lad. Quit bellyaching." He lets go, and Nack falls back against the wagon. Beck finishes up his smoke, then pours himself another tin of hot water, all careful and calm. Ain't nothing but Nack's breathing and the spit of the fire talking back to him.

"Are you up to the job, Mr. Jones?" Beck says without looking over at me.

"Yes, sir," I say. "I ain't tested the sorrel, but I can take her over at first light."

Beck looks around the camp. "Right. I'll ask for volunteers then, gentlemen."

Omer jumps up. "I'm here, Boss Beck. I'm a good swimmer. Ain't one bit scared of water. Just ask Prometheus. He knows."

Beck looks at Omer, then turns to me. "Any objections, eh?"

Omer's face is all eager with a hope I can't squelch down. I can't say no.

"We'll take a swim in the morning," I say. "All we need is a little luck."

Beck nods, and Nack gives me a bitter, hot-tempered stare. He prays for me to mess this up, I know, but I summon up all Mama's good charms in my mind until there ain't no worry demons left. Nack pushes himself up and leaves out from the fire.

Omer comes and sits beside me. "Prometheus, you going to be proud of me, I promise," he says. "I'm going to swim them beeves good as if you was working with a cowhand old as the hills. I'll do whatever you want."

"You're not going to tell me what to do?" I ask.

"No, sir, I will not. I'll be the soldier of your say. No complaints and no questions."

"Unless you don't like something."

"Well, golly molly, then I got to put things right." Omer grins. "If I don't, you know Mr. Nack will."

"Come on, then, I guess the first thing is to find you a proper horse. One that ain't fearful of water."

"You know I swim good."

"I ain't worried about you," I say. "It's General Custer we got to get across, and I ain't so sure of that sorrel. We need us a practice before we get to swimming them beeves."

By the next sunup, we've fed and corralled the saddle

strings for the day's ride, scavenged up a solid bay mare borrowed from Beck for Omer, and rode out to the river. We stand on a low ridge of coarse grass skirting the water, waiting for good daylight. We're here alone.

"Remember to let the mare have her lead," I say to Omer. "Don't grab up the reins. Let her do the thinking."

We've already stripped down to our long johns and hats, with our clothes folded neat on a solid giant of a rock, so there's nothing else to do but start swimming. The sorrel jerks nervous, but I lean in to her and sing sweet, and she takes to the shallow water.

"Stay to my right side," I say to Omer.

"I remember." I done lectured Omer all the way out here about General Custer's swimming habits, but a little reminder don't hurt none.

"And not too close. The General don't like it crowded. ..."

"I remember," Omer says.

"Always stay with your horse; grab on to her tail if you slip off. ..."

"I will!"

"And don't forget, the only thing dumber than beeves ..." I holler over the splash of the river, "is swimming beeves." The current is fast, full of twigs and leaves, and the water is a shock of cold, even with it June. The sorrel's careful with her footing but steps into the deep like some graceful dancer. She surprises me.

The horses paddle and splash and sparkle up the water like hard money jingling in your hand. I'm wet everywhere, and the teeth of morning chill bites into my lungs. But it's an alive feeling, too, and I don't fight with it.

"Wheeyee!" Omer yells. "We're riding the river!"

I look back at Omer's grin, and the moment's so pretty, it almost makes me forget my business. But the sorrel shivers and snorts a breath of water, and I remember the full charge of my responsibility.

"Don't hold on to the rein now!" I shout. "Let your horse do the swimming!"

"I ain't holding him back!" Omer follows me like a ghost rider, but I hear the aggravation in his voice.

The horses punch the water like shadowboxers. We make the island dividing the North Platte without trouble, rest the horses for a mite, then swim them on until a piece of flat, sandy bank grabs their footing. Water pours from our backs as we make shore.

"Prometheus, that was like riding a raft," Omer says. "I bet you could float back to Tennessee if you're a mind."

"Not with three thousand cattle," I say. "But you done good, Omer."

"Good as Nack?"

"Better." I don't need to tattle that Nack's scared to death of water snakes. "You're a regular fish, I'd say."

Omer beams him a smile out over the river. "Look at us, Prometheus! We's real cowboys now. Daddy Shine wouldn't believe it!"

"What makes you think he wouldn't?"

"It's a big thing to imagine is all."

Me and Omer sit there on our horses, looking out over the wide upland of prairie grass to a far ridge of rocks. The sky's still morning blue.

"You ready to swim back home?" I ask.

"Let's go," Omer answers.

"Lead the way."

When we get to camp, Ole Woman feeds us the last of the breakfast chuck with thick, hot coffee. Nack's loading up bedrolls.

"Been swimming?" he asks.

I don't say nothing, but Omer's excitement won't let him stay still. "Mr. Nack, you'd be proud of us," he says. "We done swam that river this morning and made it back here for breakfast."

"That right?"

"Yes, sir, it is."

"Is that why you're all wet?"

"Yes, sir."

"Is that why you're wet behind the ears?"

"Why, I ain't got my ears wet at all, Mr. Nack," Omer says. "Didn't even get my hat splashed up or nothing. River's running full and fast, too. Mighty pretty water. I can see why you miss it. I sure can."

Nack grunts but don't say nothing.

"You feeling poorly, Mr. Nack? I got one last piece of saltwater taffy. Been saving it for a special occasion. Might raise up your spirits and—"

Nack throws the last roll onto the wagon. "Save all your

sunshine," he says. "I don't want nothing from you."

Omer drinks up his coffee. "You don't have to want for it," he says. "I give it to you." He leaves the taffy on the rim of the wagon wheel. "A little sugar helps sweeten your day. Nip that bad feeling right in the—"

"Last thing I need is pity from a colored boy," Nack says. He don't take the candy, but he don't knock it down off the wagon wheel neither. Nack turns to me. "I guess you forgot my advice about General Custer's place around here," he says. "Cowboys are cheap, and cattle's expensive. Beck's got you working 'cause he don't mind if either of you end up with a lung full of water."

"I reckon he thinks I can handle it," I say.

"Like you handled your horse?"

"We need to hurry," I say to Omer. We hand our dishes over to Ole Woman, then push the remuda up toward the riverbank, letting them graze while we strip down again to our long johns. We'll swim the horses over first. The bawl of the herd ain't far behind us now.

Beck rides up as we mount. "Big Henry and Rio are set to hold the General until the horses are clear, lads," he says. "Let's make this an easy crossing if God's willing, gentlemen."

"We're ready, Boss Beck! We're going to take us a little walk across this water is all," Omer says. His voice is as strong as a colt's resolve.

"We're ready," I say. A tight feeling needles my gut, but the sorrel takes to the water, with the horses and Omer following. We swim back and take General Custer across without a hitch. He leads his army of bawling cattle, with me and Omer as his best lieutenants, shouting out orders in the splash and refusing retreat. The beeves swim in waves of advancing regiments, kicking hard against the current with panicky eyes.

Just as soon as we touch dry land, me and Omer swim back and start again, and by noon, most of the herd is north of the Platte. Beck and the rest of the outfit, save Rio and Big Henry, has swimmed north, too, pushing the cattle off to an open gap of ground, making room for the wet, crying beeves just finding the shore.

We swim back for the last of the stragglers, and Rio signals to hold up while he and Big Henry circle back around for any strays, so we wait.

"You ready for one last swim?" I ask Omer. We're both breathing hard, but it's the horses that pant for rest. Clouds roll up over the edge of the horizon. "A cloud's coming. Looks like we'll make it across before rain."

"With everybody safe and sound," Omer says. "Mr. Nack didn't need to worry you like he did."

"He never worried me," I say. "All we needed was a little luck. Looks like we got it."

Omer grins. "I swear, you *is* the luckiest child on earth, Prometheus Jones."

A band of a hundred or so ill-tempered beeves comes toward us. Rio and Big Henry whip the ends of their ropes along the cattle's backsides, moving them toward the water. I pull my hat down. "I hope you're right about that," I say. "But let's finish this up before our luck dries up for the day. Might be lightning in that storm."

We get the beeves to swimming. Rio leads and I follow behind, with Big Henry and Omer off to our left. We're halfway to the island, when something unknown sets three or four cattle in a panic.

They turn and fight with the current. A commotion sets up among the animals, and water splashes wild in our faces. Rio and I swim into the middle of the uproar and whip our ropes on the river, trying to draw the beeves back on course. But the current pulls us along quick, and the ropes get tangled up in the thrashing. Rio's under and up again, and I'm penned between two bellowing heifers, both kicking furious against the fast-moving water. All we can do is push forward and hope the beeves find ground before they tire out and drown us all.

Off to my side, Big Henry and Omer are jumbled shoulder to shoulder against a mass of animals in a full panic. I press my knees into the sorrel's sides to try and get back to them. A jittery shiver passes through the horse. She's strong-headed and won't fight the current and cattle sweeping us along. Within a minute, one of the heifers falls back, drops below the surface of the water, and is gone. I nudge the horse in the ribs to turn to the drowning beeve; Omer and Big Henry will have to take care of themselves. Beck won't tolerate a loss to the herd, not even a stubborn heifer.

Big Henry hollers out to me, but I can't hear him. My back is turned from Omer, and the current rides us along too fast to keep our bearings. Suddenly, the downed heifer bursts up, wetting us both in her spray. I breathe water in through my nose. A burning catches in my throat, and I gag up the taste of mud.

Big Henry hollers out again, but I'm caught and can't hear. The beeves bob and bawl themselves into a rush of trouble. We've pushed them along toward a sliver of solid ground at the edge of the island, but there's not enough land to hold up.

"Push them on!" I yell. "Can't hold them here!"

Rio whistles loud and whips his rope across the beeves' backs. His horse is out of the water on the island and back in the river on the other side before the beeves have a chance to slow. The first animals find the mud of the island's shore, and I fling my rope against the rump of a stubborn steer to keep it moving forward. The sorrel ain't found footing yet, and the splash and the cry of the beeves fill up my ears. But there's another sound, too.

Big Henry yells again. He swims downriver from us, fighting hard against the flow of the current. I know from his manner something ain't right. I call behind me to Omer for help. But when I look back, the water swirls into nothing but a stirred-up foam of muck and grass. I search out over the beeves. Can't see Omer anywhere—not behind me, not in front of me neither. His bay is gone, too. I dig my heel into the sorrel's side and force a turn back toward Big Henry and slap out my rope for him to grab on.

He calls out first. "Omer's underwater!" he yells. "Can't find him!"

Big Henry follows Rio and gets the beeves to the far shore. I turn back. Ripples fan out as the sorrel splashes up to her withers. Nothing stirs from below. No bubbles along the waterline. No fish bobbing about. The wind picks up, but I swim out into the deepest part of the river. Omer's missing, but he'll turn up just like Nack. He'll pop up, and I'll catch him and pound the water out of his lungs and scold him for holding on too tight to the bay.

I push the sorrel up and down the river until the horse is almost give out with tired. Again. And again. And again. Still nothing.

Rain comes up fast. Rio hands off the cattle and swims back across to join in the search. We swim until after dark, hunting along the riverbank, hollering out for Omer. But our voices echo unanswered in the drumming rain. Finally, Beck comes down and tells us to quit. We can't do no good in the dark. We'll look for the body in the morning. I don't follow orders. Neither does Rio. But sometime before midnight, Beck coaxes us out of the water.

I can't feel nothing, not the wet cold, not the sour taste coming up from my gut, not the hot coffee Ole Woman forces on me. I huddle up under a wet tarp by a smoking fire in damp long johns with my knees tight up under my chin to wait for the sun.

Come daybreak, Nack starts up the coffee while I bridle the sorrel to go back out into the water.

"How you like being a cowboy now?" he says. "I done told you a man's life is cheap when compared to beeves. You done right by letting him drown. Probably saved Beck three or four heifers."

"Hush up, old man," I say in a whisper. "Can't you just hush up for once?" Our eyes lock, and shame fills up Nack's face. He don't say no more.

"Over here!" I run when Rio hollers.

The whole outfit joins the search, and within an hour of daybreak, Omer's body is found under a shelf of washed-out bank. He looks small now, like a little boy ready to climb in bed after playing in the yard. His hat's gone, but he's wearing his long johns, and his whip is tied to his waist in a coil. His face is bloated and purple from spending the night in the river.

"Leave him be," I say to Rio. I jump down into the muck and weeds and clutch Omer's wet body to my chest. His skin is cold and slippery, and the mud and leaves from his face and hair stick to my shirt.

"Wake up! Wake up! Homer Lovejoy Shine, I'm talking to you! You hear me?" I yell. I shake him hard. "Get up now! Get up! Come on!"

Rio reaches out with a firm grip on my hand. "Easy, my friend," he whispers. "Omer cannot hear you now."

A wild beast howl comes up out of me. "No, no, no, no, no ... don't let it be!" I cling on to Omer, hugging him like my mama did when he was a baby. “Mama! Mama! Don’t let it be! Don’t let it be!” But life is flowed out of Omer like that river.

“Mama! Please ... Mama ... please ... please ...” My voice bellows out, and I rock Omer’s body back and forth until it slips from my hands to the ground, and I double up over it. “Mama ... please ... please.”

But she don’t hear my voice, and there ain’t nothing but mud and the stench of death. Omer’s with Mama now.

“Wrap the corpse in a pony blanket, lads,” Beck says so quiet I almost don’t hear. “Let’s get back to camp.”

Omer is lost. And it’s my curse to be alive.

CHAPTER SEVENTEEN

We say good-bye to a cowboy.

We never find Omer's horse. Beck thinks the bay got tangled in his reins, and Omer tried to free it.

"It's God's plan on earth," Beck says. "We can't know why."

"A service … I got to give Omer a service," I say. "I can't send word to Daddy Shine without …" My voice sinks, and I can't think of words.

Beck nods. "We'll hold up for the day," he says.

Ole Woman helps me dress Omer's body in his best shirt and pants, then tie it tight in the pony blanket. He cuts a lock of hair for me to send to Daddy Shine once we reach Deadwood. I keep his whip. It's stiff with river water, but I can't bear to part with it.

Big Henry and Tuttle help scout for a resting place. We don't have a proper coffin, but Rio and me dig a deep hole on a little ridge of land overlooking the river, not far from camp. We line it with small stones, then lay Omer's body down neat and clean on the rocks. We cover it with dirt, then two of the boys haul a good-sized piece of sandstone over it, and I scratch *Homer Lovejoy Shine* out with Ole Woman's knife. The whole outfit stands there silent. Even Nack don't have no words.

The river water dances along in the sun without regrets, and nothing keeps the day from shining out in its glory. Ain't no magic can keep Omer from crossing into the next world, but Mama never warned me about his drowning. If I hadn't gone after that heifer, would Omer still be alive?

"Didn't know if anybody wanted to say a few words," Tuttle says. He wipes his nose on the back of his hand. "Don't have a Bible, but thought I'd say a piece. Memorized it a year or so back ..." He clears his throat and stares out into the distance.

> *"When God gets to worrying where his handiwork lay,*
> *He remembers a cowpuncher's soul keeps the day.*
> *Roaming the prairie, tending God's herd,*
> *Working the land, and keeping his word.*
> *Finding God's grace in all that he sees,*
> *Till God stops his worrying, and all is at ease."*

A gust of wind blows up a little whirlwind of dirt. Beck says the Lord's Prayer, then puts on his hat. "Godspeed, Mr. Shine," he says.

I stand there looking at the dirt and stone. Finally, Beck pats me on the shoulder and walks back to camp. Big Henry and Tuttle and the rest of the boys drift on off after him. It ain't long until it's just me and Rio grieving there at Omer's tombstone.

"Sleep well, amigo," Rio says to Omer, then turns to me. "You coming, Prometheus Jones?"

"Why didn't I leave that heifer to drown?" I ask.

"Blame does not change what happens," Rio says. "Beck was right. We cannot know God's will. Omer is in heaven with my twin sons, and they are all in a better place."

My eyes throb in the bright blue of the morning sky. "You really think there is a heaven?"

"Sí, amigo, sí. Come now." We walk back to camp, and I sit and watch the fire while the outfit eats noon grub. Ole Woman offers me a thick bean-and-meat stew, but the food is without taste. The camp is somber and dull. Con plays a tune on his harp to settle the cattle, but the afternoon heat does just as well. The herd is lazy and worn.

Before evening, Beck rides over to Camp Clarke. "We need an extra hand," he says, "and an extra gun. Tomorrow, we'll head north."

Rio asks me to write a letter to his wife, and I take down the words. All my hope of going to Texas and finding my pappy seems vanished now.

Beck rides in at dark with Mr. Wheeler and Donahue. They are back in our company as hired guns, with Donahue our guide. "Rest up, lads," Beck orders up. "We will make a full day of it tomorrow."

Mr. Wheeler offers up his condolences. "There is a silver lining in these unfortunate events, Mr. Jones," he says.

"The Lakota call this part of the country sacred ground as I understand. ..."

"Who's the Lakota?" I ask.

"Part of the Sioux nation," Mr. Wheeler says. "A distinct tribe, I believe. At least that is the perception of the barkeep in Camp Clarke. So I should think this ground has been pristine for hundreds, if not thousands, of years. And as such, I'm sure your cousin will rest well here."

"I appreciate the notion, Mr. Wheeler," I say.

"Why, I should wish to be buried in just such beautiful country myself," Mr. Wheeler continues.

"Well, don't wish too hard," Donahue says. "I ain't of a mind to die anytime soon, and I'm stuck with you until we get to Deadwood."

I leave Mr. Wheeler and Donahue arguing at the fire, unroll my bed, and pull off my boots. I can't bear to go through Omer's things just yet. Ole Woman says they'll be a time for that later. I pull Mama's paper from my hat. Mr. Jones seems a long ways off now. And now Omer is lost, too. A loneliness washes up over me, wide and empty.

We move the cattle at sunrise, holding the herd tight and keeping steady watch. If we stick together and set a solid pace, Beck says we might sneak past the Sioux. Donahue ain't so hopeful and tells Beck to be ready to barter some beeves for passage through Buffalo Gap. Every man in the outfit has his iron loaded and strapped to his belt.

Beck don't let me loll about none saying my good-byes. By the time the string horses are watered and ready for saddling, Beck is pushing us to head out. I wait until the wagon is packed, then circle back and draw a good-luck star in the dirt over Omer's grave and cut a line through it with my finger, just like Mama taught me.

"You were my good cousin, Omer," I whisper into the dawn. "Forgive me. . . . I didn't know you were in trouble. . . ." A knot of regret winds itself around my heart. "Ain't nothing on earth can separate us, though. I ain't ever forgetting."

"You coming?" It's Nack. He's learned the rhythm of his walking crutch; I didn't hear him come up behind me.

"Thought about it."

"I got something of yours," he says. He pitches a piece of saltwater taffy in the air, and I catch it in my hand. "That sidekick of yours gave this to me yesterday. Said it was his last piece, but it might help raise my spirits. Figure you could use it now."

"You trying to feel better about treating Omer so poorly?"

Nack's jaw sets hard. "I don't need no guff from you," he says. He turns to walk back. "And I'll just keep my condolences to myself."

I squeeze the taffy in my hand. "I tried to save the heifer and . . ."

Nack turns back. "And your cousin drowned. Life's full of bad luck, boy. Better learn that." He walks on toward camp. "Best get going. Tell Ole Woman I'll be there directly."

I don't say nothing but pull myself into my saddle. I open my hand and smell the sweet sugar of the taffy, then throw it far into the grass. All my luck is done soured.

CHAPTER EIGHTEEN

We travel on to Buffalo Gap.

We're eight days north and no sign of Indians, and not much water neither. The grass has given way to snake-weed, and the cattle moan hungry and worrisome, but Beck says we'll reach the south fork of the Cheyenne River tomorrow. He's anxious for news from the Fort Peck outfit set to meet us outside Deadwood. Two days back, the agent at the Red Cloud Indian Agency laughed when Beck said we was taking the herd through Buffalo Gap.

"Might as well shoot every animal yourself," he said. "There's a war brewing with the Sioux, or haven't you heard?"

But Beck ain't ruffled. "I'll keep to my plan," he says. "Suppose that makes me a betting man, then, eh?"

The agent's a tall thin fellow named Saville, and he don't take to Beck's bravado. "You can bet your life you won't make it halfway there. Get yourself killed is all. No enterprise is worth your scalp."

"We'll take the herd and deliver it, sir, and my enter-prise will make me a wealthy man," Beck says in a harsh voice. But Beck's a practical man, too, and he takes on a train of three prospector wagons and another eight men to ride along with us once we leave Red Cloud. They're as pleased for our protection as we are for theirs.

Every day, we meet folks heading south out of Dakota Territory. Most are down-and-out gold miners, but we meet families, too, and rough-looking characters that Donahue eyes with trigger-finger nerves. That don't keep Mr. Wheeler from questioning every man, woman, and child we meet and hearing their tales of hard luck, Indian scalpings, and gold claims. Mr. Wheeler writes every tiny detail in that notebook of his.

Donahue swears the Sioux is trailing us, so Beck sends Rio and Tuttle back to help me keep up with the stragglers. The ground is more rocky now. We're a tight band: horses, cattle, wagons, and men.

Rio don't seem vexed about the Sioux. "Fear will kill a man before the Indians will," he says. "Besides, within a fortnight the herd will be delivered. We will have wages, a warm bed, and a hot meal. Perhaps a drink of Cutter to celebrate, no? I will have a letter from my wife, and you will have your news regarding Irwin."

But since Omer's passing, I ain't cared much about finding Mr. Jones. If I look for him and never find him, I'll be more alone in the world than I can bear. Better off not to know.

Work is back-breaking hard. Beck declares a double-watch and no campfires after dark. Not a man in the outfit sleeps more than a spell of an hour all night, and the next morning, we're up following roving clouds by the time the sun shows her light.

Midafternoon, the cattle smell the water of the Cheyenne, even though it's not much more than a creek. The herd hurries toward the bank, but before we get a good watering, a band of five Sioux come riding up.

Beck heads out to meet them, and Donahue sends a whistle out man-to-man for warning. I rest my hand near my Colt, round up the remuda into a tight circle of horseflesh, and wait.

The Sioux is mostly dressed in buckskin breechcloth with shawls wound around their legs to form breeches. Their braided hair is wrapped in animal skins, with dark red stripes painted down the parts of their scalps. But one Indian wears a slouch hat, yellow trousers, and a bright-colored calico shirt. He looks older than the other Sioux. I can hear him speaking English to Beck; their voices hang on the wind over the cries of the beeves. The Sioux ain't interested in trading with the prospectors, he says, but he talks in a strong voice until finally Beck pulls a paper out of his saddlebag and hands it to the Sioux. The Sioux don't even open it, but he hands it back to Beck. They set to arguing again.

I dry my sweaty hands along my dungarees. Silver metal gleams off the Sioux's shotgun, and I'm ready to reach for my Colt.

"Prometheus Jones!" Beck motions me over to him. "Prometheus Jones!"

I hand off the remuda to Tuttle and press my heels into the sorrel's sides.

"We have a little issue of diplomacy, Mr. Jones," Beck says. "There's a bit of tittle-tattle among the lads that you read. Is that the God's truth?"

I look at the Sioux close up. Shell earrings decorate their ears, and two have bracelets and armlets over wool shirts. All of the Sioux are armed, some with cartridges and pistols, as well as shotguns.

"I read well as some," I say.

"Read," the Indian says. "Read Trail Boss paper."

Beck turns his horse and speaks in a low voice to me. "It's the government purchase order from Fort Peck," Beck says. "Our Indian brethren here want a hundred beeves to let us cross their land," Beck says. "I told him the whole herd was on order from Fort Peck for winter beef to feed the Sioux. They take from me now, they'll be taking from the mouths of women and children. But he doesn't trust me reading the order, says he wants you. Trusts your word more than mine," Beck says.

"Why? I ain't no—"

"The color of your skin, Mr. Jones," Beck says. I hear the irritation in his voice. "I don't have a Fairy Flag's clue what the Indian is thinking. I just want him to understand so we can move on out of here. Read, sir."

I take up the paper and read it loud, stumbling over some of the fancy words. The Sioux listens, and by that time, Donahue has joined us as well.

"'. . . Signed here by Seamus Beck, boss for the Diamond Dot Ranch, and Jack Simmons, Agent, Fort Peck Indian Agency. March 13, 1876.'"

"Don't matter what any paper says," Donahue speaks to the Indians. "You're already considered hostiles by the United States Government for not being on your reservation. Something happens to this outfit, and the U.S. Army will come after you."

"Hold your tongue, Mr. Donahue," Beck says. "You gave me your word to contain yourself."

"And they'll shoot down every one of you. And your women and children, too."

"I said hold your tongue, sir!" Beck yells.

"Why, I might not wait for the government. I might start shooting right now. We're twenty-guns strong, and I don't think you boys are up for a fight." Donahue pulls his Colt fast, cocks the trigger, and aims at the old Indian in the yellow trousers.

"Put your gun down, Mr. Donahue," Beck yells.

"I will not. You may think these heathens are good to their word, but you're an innocent when it comes to their kind. Force is all they understand."

"Put down your gun." Beck talks slow and quiet now. Beck's eyes is glowing like a lightning fire. He might kill Donahue before the Indians have a chance.

The Sioux looks me over, glares down hard at Donahue, then nods to the others in his band. "We go," he says.

"I'll cut out five beeves, one for each of you," Beck offers.

Donahue uncocks his iron. “Pleasure doing business with you, boys,” he says to the Indians. Donahue has a smirk on his face that comes from some evil place inside him. He rides back toward the prospectors.

“Mr. Jones, get Big Henry and cut out the cattle,” Beck says.

“We take own cattle,” the Indian says. “We pick—”

“No,” Beck says. His voice is firm. “We’ll give you the cattle. It would be disrespectful if I ask you to pick out your own gifts, my brethren. Wait and we will bring them to you.” Beck looks at me. We both know he wants to hand over the worst of our herd.

Beck stays while me and Big Henry round up five ailing heifers. We bring them over.

“You will feast tonight,” Beck says. “Fine cattle.” He nods. “Fine meat.”

“Great white father lies to Lakota. All white men lie,” the Indian says. He takes the beeves, then turns and rides with the band and the animals along the ridge.

Beck, Big Henry, and me watch them go. “They needed the food,” Beck says. “A Sioux warrior won’t back down from a fool’s loud mouth without cause.”

Suddenly, a gunshot burns past us and stirs the horses. Donahue is back among the prospectors, their guns drawn to the man. Laughter recoils off the rocks. Donahue waves his Colt in the air. “Run, you dogs!” he says. “Run! We ain’t scared of no savages!” He shoots again.

Beck hightails it over to Donahue and just as he reaches

the men, another shot rings out and sends Donahue from his horse. I turn and see the Sioux in the yellow trousers lower his shotgun and disappear down a gully.

"Hold up!" Beck hollers out to the men. "Hold up! Don't fire!"

Ole Woman and Mr. Wheeler kneel down over the body. "He's dead—shot through the heart," Ole Woman says. "That Indian was aiming right for him."

Words fly from the prospectors, but not one of them is brave enough to chase down after the Sioux.

"Dear Lord in heaven!" Mr. Wheeler says as he pulls a fine white linen shirt from his saddlebag to cover Donahue's face. "We're going to end up bald, every one of us," he says.

"All we can do now is get going," Beck says. "Get the cattle watered, and we'll move on to Buffalo Gap before dark. Hustle, gentlemen, we can't afford to stay now."

"We can't just leave Mr. Donahue for the vultures and vermin!" Mr. Wheeler says. "It isn't Christian, Mr. Beck. Not Christian at all."

"I suppose you're right, Mr. Wheeler," Beck says. "So, I elect you to stay behind and dig Mr. Donahue's grave. I'm sure you want to do your Christian duty, eh?"

"Well, I don't . . ." Wheeler's face is red as a plum.

"Then, you'll kindly get on your horse and shut your mouth," Beck says. "Oh, and Mr. Wheeler . . ."

"Yes?"

"Take Donahue's Colt and ammunition off him. We'll need them if I'm a betting man."

"Well, I'll do no such ..."

Ole Woman unbuckles Donahue's gun belt.

"Nack, can you ride, sir?" Beck asks.

"Just give me a horse."

"Take Donahue's weapon and mount, then, and ride with Mr. Jones. They'll be eyeing our horses now," Beck says. "Let's go, gentlemen!"

Beck rides to the front of the herd and snaps his rope at General Custer, then signals to push the cattle off the Cheyenne. The prospectors saddle up and crack their whips at the oxen. We're moving north.

But so are the Sioux.

CHAPTER NINETEEN

We make a run for Deadwood.

We take our evening meal of jerked buffalo while we mount a change of horses. It's midnight before we make the entrance to Buffalo Gap. Beck presses to go on, but the prospectors refuse, so we hold up for sleep until the sun shows her light. I take first watch as nighthawk but give in to Nack soon as watch is called. I sleep fully clothed with my holster for my pillow, but I'm so tired it ain't long until I'm dreaming.

In my vision, no words of comfort come from Mama. I swim the river over and over, but Omer's not there. I call out to him. But he don't answer. My temper gets heated, and I curse out against Omer and Mama and God and fate. But my voice just echoes lonely in my ears. Does Mama know the truth? Omer's dead because of me.

Rio calls me awake.

"You are searching for Omer in your sleep," Prometheus Jones," Rio says. "*Ven.* Sit with me. It is better than fighting your dreams."

I pull my blanket around my shoulders and grab my

hat. The night is still and dark, with the red fire of Rio's cigarette our only light.

"Your grief visits your sleep, Prometheus Jones?" Rio asks. "*Eso es malo.*"

"Can't help it," I say.

We sit quiet for a long time until Rio speaks in a low, soft voice.

"I could not get the doctor to come when my sons fell sick," he says. "Many children were dying. At first my boys wouldn't eat, but soon they were filled with pains in their bellies. We piled the bed with blankets, but they shivered in fever. ..."

Rio breathes out smoke and night air. "My wife fed them like birds—spoonfuls of onion soup—and bathed them in wet rags. But they vomited the soup, and their faces burned hot. Their eyes turned yellow. By the next morning, the vomit was blood, and the screams ... the screams." He sighs. "I could not stand the screams, so I ran out of the house." He stubs the end of his cigarette out under his boot. "That night, my wife came to the saloon and brought me home. But my sons were dead."

I can't think of no good words of comfort. I rock forward and hold my stomach to keep my feelings inside. "Reckon they was all better once they got to heaven," I say. "Ain't no sick angels."

"Death is a merciless master, my friend. We cannot keep it from the ones we love."

Grief crushes around my throat. "But ... but I could

have saved him. ..." I breathe faster now, and my eyes fill up with water. "I just didn't know. ... I didn't take care. ..." The words squeeze the air out of my chest.

"Give in to your grief, my friend," Rio says. "You will not be less of a man if you own your heart."

My heart breaks open, and a flood of tears comes up out of my gut. Cries shake out of me. I cry for Good Eye. And for Omer. And for Mama. And for Mr. Jones, who never came looking for me.

Rio takes a long drink from the flask in his vest pocket. Light is creeping its way toward morning. I cry till there ain't nothing left—till my insides is empty. Rio sits and waits. Finally, I blow my nose into my kerchief, pull my blanket hard around me, and stare at the ground.

"You do not see it now, my friend, but you are a lucky man, Prometheus Jones," Rio says. "Your grief will help you remember how to love."

"How do you mean?" I whisper.

"For all their words and tempers, Nack and Beck are men I trust," Rio says. "But they have let hard times harden their hearts. But you, Prometheus Jones, you are young. You will find your way to a happy life. ..."

"But everything got messed up, and I ain't even sure I'll find—"

"Who do you seek through Irwin?" Rio asks.

My voice splinters saying the words out loud. "My pappy."

Rio waits for me.

I pull Mama's paper out of my hat. "My mama done told me he got sold into Texas before I was born, but we never heard from him after the war. When she died, she made me promise I'd go look for him, but I ain't even sure he's alive." I throw the paper down. "He probably don't even want no son."

"You cannot know that." Rio picks up the paper and hands it to me, then rolls another cigarette.

"I don't know much of nothing."

"We seldom do, my friend. That is life, no?" Rio strikes a match and his face shines familiar, but his eyes are tired like the eyes of old soldiers after the war. "My wife still sends a letter in Deadwood," he says. "Will you read it?"

"If you want."

"*Gracias,* amigo. News to cheer us both up, perhaps?"

We don't talk no more. The camp begins to stir, and Nack brings up the string horses. Mr. Wheeler looks for Beck, and the prospectors gather round one of the wagons for a meeting. The sky is full of clouds. By the time I've got my bedroll packed, Beck rides up, ready to go with a new plan.

"We're going to make a run for it, gentlemen," he says. "We'll stop for a bit of rest, but we won't make full camp until Deadwood." Beck raises his voice over the prospectors' protests. "This plan is risky, gentlemen, but it's our best chance to outwit any trouble from Mr. Donahue's ill-timed bragging."

"But how much of a run can we make with three

thousand cattle, Mr. Beck?" Wheeler asks. "It seems perilous to try to run!"

"I don't see that we have much of a choice, sir," Beck says. "Going will be slow, but at least we'll be a moving target."

The prospectors grumble and groan, but finally agree.

"Be vigilant." Beck nods, then saddles his horse. His words don't hide the unease in his voice. "We can't afford to be stupid, gentlemen. And you might offer up a little prayer, Mr. Wheeler."

The clouds warn of rain all morning. Nack rides with Ole Woman to rest while I take the remuda and ride drag with Tuttle. Beck and Big Henry scout up ahead, while Rio and Con keep General Custer moving forward. Beck is right. Things is mighty slow going.

We see signs of Indians everywhere. Not so much the Indians themselves as a trail of discarded clothes, tools, and wagons left by white folks running to escape an Indian scalping knife. We don't see no bodies until midday. There's a man who looked to be a prospector shot in the forehead. The stench of his dead body announces him to us, but we don't take the time to bury him proper. Mr. Wheeler don't protest this time.

The cattle ain't no trouble, so we plod along. But shortly, Big Henry rides back into our company with news of a Sioux war party up ahead.

"Lakota, best I can tell. I spied seventeen of them. Camped about three miles up in the hills, overlooking the gap," Big Henry says. "But something's odd. Their ponies are tuckered out, and my guess is they been traveling fast. Seen some scalps on them, and most got Henry rifles. I saw one Spencer."

"They'll pick us off like wild turkeys," one of the prospectors says.

"We'll never get past them," another one yells.

"I should say not!" Mr. Wheeler takes out his handkerchief and pats the sweat off his lip. "This is a fine situation you have us in, Mr. Beck. Just what do you propose we do now?"

"Nothing yet," Beck says. "Let's get the herd situated best we can, then peruse our options."

A soft rain starts up like a godsend, so we settle the cattle on a narrow strip of grass without too much struggle. The prospectors are jittery and ready for Beck's answers.

"What say we negotiate?" one of the prospectors shouts.

"They wouldn't trade with you yesterday, man, so what makes you think they will now?" Beck answers. "I'll offer up cattle, but I don't know if that will appease them."

"You ready to give up more than a hundred head?" Nack asks. "They won't settle for a pittance."

"Let's surprise them hostiles and kill every one of them!" another man orders.

"We don't have the firepower!" Beck says.

"You don't have the guts!"

Beck's aggravation gleams out over the prospectors. "At least I'm not a bloody idiot!"

"We're going to die right here in this infernal gap," Mr. Wheeler says. "I should have listened to my publisher and never come to this wilderness."

Voices break into a dozen shouts until Beck about draws his Colt. "Gentlemen, discipline yourselves," he says. "We cannot attack these Lakota, but we can't hope for survival on a lick and a promise. We need a plan, sirs."

"I got a plan." I speak my words before I realize I done opened my mouth. "You say them Lakota is tuckered out? I know something that might work."

"Eh? Tell us what you're thinking." Beck's voice is matter of fact.

"When you hired me on, Mr. Beck, you said you served with the Ohio regiment in Tennessee. You run with Schofield?"

"General Schofield?"

"Were you with him when he marched past Hood at Spring Hill? Ain't a Negro in Tennessee don't know that story. Big Henry said them Sioux is all tired out, just like them Johnny Rebs. Think that might work here?"

Beck stops and pulls on his mustache. "Sneak a train of wagons and cattle by the Lakota in the middle of the night?"

"If it starts raining hard, they might not hear us," I say. "We could keep watch on them and send out an alarm if they get wind of our plot."

Beck's eyes dance for a moment. "That's a bully good idea, Mr. Jones!"

"What exactly do you propose, Mr. Beck?" Wheeler asks, "waltzing right past the Lakota in plain sight?"

"Them Sioux ain't a bunch of weak-willed graybacks," Nack says. "They'll skin us alive!"

"Dear Lord in heaven!" Mr. Wheeler looks more pale than normal. "This is madness, Mr. Beck."

"It's ingenious! Gentlemen, we'll wait for cover of dark, then post lookouts. We can tie canvas to muffle the sound of the wagons and the horses. The rain will help us even more. Perhaps we can move our whole herd and your wagons through the gap without our Indian brethren even aware of us."

"And what if they hear us?"

"Then we'll have a fight on our hands, lads," Beck says. "What do you say, now? If you've a mind to stay behind, I won't go forcing my point. You're welcome to go it alone."

Ain't a man in the group willing to do that, so Beck shouts out orders, and we toil well into the evening to cut the canvas from the wagons and tie it to the horses' hooves and the wagon wheels. We'll keep the cattle to the soft ground as best we can.

After dark, the black sky opens up, and it rains full and steady. The sorrel is calm and sure-footed, so I pull my oilcloth coat tight around me, tilt my head back, and catch some raindrops in my mouth. The rain is cold and clean. I call out to Mama in my mind, and I catch her voice on the wind. *Lucky child.*

Beck sends Big Henry and Con to watch and signal

with two rapid gunshots if the Indians discover us. "We need to work quick and quiet, men," Beck says, and with that, we start. Nack takes the remuda up front, and me and Rio ride drag.

We move slow and silent less than a half mile from the Indian camp and in their full view. The night and the rain stain the country like ink. Not a man in the outfit talks or breathes deep, and there's no whistling out to the cattle.

The beeves fuss about, but Ole Woman offers Beck a gunnysack of feed to lure General Custer, and soon the herd finds a steady pace. The drone of the rain seems to soothe their jaded nerves.

Within three hours, every horse, beeve, and wagon is north of the Lakota camp, and Big Henry and Con are back in our company. By morning we've pushed on to Custer, but Beck don't stop. The cattle is only a might worrisome, and on the fourth morning, we reach Deadwood, whipped and bleary-eyed, but alive.

"Hallelujah, Hallelujah," Mr. Wheeler says. "We are amongst the living." He gets off his horse and kneels down on the ground. "I do think we owe our very existence to that Negro boy there. Prometheus Jones, you are a resourceful young man, and just as soon as I am presentable, I'm going straight to the hotel and have a glass of claret in your honor!"

Deadwood lies at the bottom of a ravine rimmed by a slim valley of trees so green they show black to the eye. The prospectors work their wagons with ropes and muscle down the steep grade of winding road to the town's main stretch of street, filled with wagons, men, and mud.

The cattle settle on a ridge of pasture overlooking Deadwood. From a distance, the weathered clapboard buildings of the town scar the deep green of the hills. There ain't no mansions and no silver dishes, but my heart is as eager as if the streets were lined with gold. Down there somewhere is a letter with news of my pappy.

CHAPTER TWENTY

The past catches up with me.

Beck heads off to Stebbins, Post & Co. Bank to ask after Jack Simmons and the sale of the herd and returns by dark with a smile wider than a white preacher man.

"Cheers to us," he says, holding up his tin and pouring two fingers of new-bought whiskey into his cup. "Mr. Simmons and his company will come for the herd at sunup. We'll do a tally, and you gents can head into Deadwood for a bath and a bed and some milling about. As for me, I might take in a good meal. There's tell in town of a little lady who fries a wondrous lamb chop."

Ole Woman frowns, but Beck just grins, and Ole Woman shakes his head and throws his cigar into the fire.

"From what I see, Deadwood's a regular high society, eh?" Beck teases. "There's a bona fide theater with a fine baritone and a pretty soprano and a hurdy-gurdy establishment for you dancing boys. They were already playing cards this morning at the sporting house next to the outfitter's." Horseplay sparks in Beck's eyes. "So take a day to spend your fortunes, lads, then be ready to ride with me after that. I'll be selling the wagon and the remuda and settling up my affairs, then heading to Texas, and I won't be waiting on you."

"What day is it?" Tuttle asks. "I done lost count."

"July 3," Beck says. "Monday. Scuttlebutt is, Deadwood's hosting a centennial celebration tomorrow in honor of a little slip of paper signed in Philadelphia, so you won't lack for amusements. But business first, so let's get to it, eh?"

We sort the supplies and get the cattle bedded down for the evening, but the grass is thin, and the herd bellows hungry during the night. Beck calls up a full watch, and we count the stars, eager for morning.

At dawn, Simmons shows up with a dozen ragtag cowboys, and we set about tallying the herd. When everyone's happy, Beck settles our pay.

"Don't spend this all in one place," Beck tells me as he hands me my wages. I offer up to him that I've a mind to purchase the sorrel for my own, and he agrees. "And if you're still interested, lad, you're welcome to ride south with us."

"I'm beholden to you, Mr. Beck," I say. "I guess that's always been my plan."

By noon, I'm riding into Deadwood with Rio and Con and Big Henry. Happy as this day ought to be, a bittersweet taste hangs up in my throat. I got to send Daddy Shine word about Omer.

"What are you going to name that horse of yours?" Rio asks.

"Don't have a name as yet," I say. "Figure one will come to me. Can't think of it now."

"Are you headed for the outfitter's?" Rio asks. "I am going there to look for mail from my bride." He smiles but don't ask me nothing more.

"I got to send a letter to Daddy Shine," I say.

"Then we shall go together, my friend."

Deadwood's main street is a river of wagons, horses, coarse-looking men, fancied-up gamblers, prospectors, and a few honest faces. A tall liberty pole with rough-sewn flags beautifies the street for the centennial celebration.

We stop a staunch-built fellow to ask for directions to the outfitter's, and he tells us to head for the corner of Main and Lee streets and look for a moon-shaped sign: Zion's Cooperative Mercantile Institution. It's sure a smart name for nothing more than a dry goods store.

In front of the building, a sandy blonde man dressed in a fine jacket speaks to a crowd of men. "... opening for settlement the country we are now occupying and improving. Further, that the government, for which we offered our lives, at once extend a protecting arm and take us under its care."

The crowd makes a big noise of applause, and a prospector whistles out his good cheer.

"Sign this petition, my fellow citizens," the man says, "and this territory shall soon be part of that mighty republic, the United States of America." The men give their say-so with more clapping and slaps on each other's backs and jolly-good-fellow laughter. Mr. Wheeler is amongst the men. He jots down words from the speech.

"This is a most exciting turn of events," Mr. Wheeler says. "Most exciting! Have you seen Mr. Beck?"

"He is still back at camp, Señor Wheeler," Rio says. "But he will not be long in coming to town. He mentioned interest in a hot meal."

"The people of the Black Hills are calling for an official territory, and what with the annihilation of General Custer, it will be the devil if the government doesn't come and protect—"

"General Custer? The hero General Custer?" I ask.

Mr. Wheeler looks funny for a moment. "The general himself! Haven't you heard the news?"

"*¿Qué ha pasado?*" Rio asks. "What is it?"

"General Custer and the Seventh Cavalry were cut to pieces by Lakota Sioux and Cheyenne braves west of here at Little Big Horn. Happened two weeks ago."

"Where are the Indians now?" Rio asks.

"On the run, according to the army," Wheeler says. "Some slipped into Canada, but it won't take long to track them down. The Indians may have won the battle, but the government won't lose the war." Mr. Wheeler's face flushes. "I just have to tell Mr. Beck it is my theory that the Indians we passed in Buffalo Gap were part of that very same warring party. What else could make more sense? Didn't your scout say their horses were worn out? They obviously didn't want to make themselves known for fear of reprisal. I say we were heavens-to-Betsy lucky. Can you imagine our good fortune out of this tragedy?"

"I will say prayers for General Custer and his men," Rio says. "I am sure Beck will come to the hotel if you want to wait."

Mr. Wheeler nods and rushes off.

"Think it was the same Indians?" I ask as we enter the outfitter's.

"Does it matter, my friend?" Rio says. "We were still lucky, no?"

Inside, I buy some paper and write out a letter for Daddy Shine, but the words is hard. I tell him Omer's with Mama, and I know Daddy Shine will take comfort in that. I send along Omer's pay and a lock of his hair.

Rio waits for me, and I hold on to my breath 'cause he don't have a letter from Texas in his hand. No news. But the mail from Rapid City won't be in until tomorrow, he says, so we meander about the store until Rio settles on a drink of whiskey in the gaming hall next door.

"Two bits," the barkeep says. He don't even ask me what I'm drinking, but I ain't drinking whiskey so it don't matter. Two dried-up pieces of saltwater taffy sit in a jar next to the liquor. I buy the candy and chew on the hard sugar of it.

"You boys staying around for the Champion of the West Extravaganza?" the barkeep asks.

"Don't know about it," I say.

"Contest is open to any man, woman, or child in Deadwood. Five dollars to enter, but a hundred-dollar prize for the Champion of the West with the best shooting and riding," he says as he drops our coins into his cashbox. "The Extravaganza part is a dance afterward with some of the girls at the Gem Theater. Don't know if you would enjoy the dancing, but you boys look like cowboys to me. Might have a chance at that prize money. Don't think they got rules against Negroes and Mexicans long as you got the entry money."

"Where do we pay, amigo?" Rio asks.

"Down at the livery," the barkeep says. "But you better hurry. Things are starting up this afternoon."

Rio looks at me. "You must enter. You have a sharp eye and a confident hand, and there is no man who can best your talents with horseflesh, agreed? I will bet on you, and we will both be rich men."

"I might could win it."

Rio tips his head back and the whiskey slips down his throat. "Let us join in the festivities. We will go and take a look."

A host of men stand outside the livery. Big Henry is there from camp, already signed up. Nack sits on an old barrel drinking from his flask.

"Don't care two bits about the contest," Big Henry says. "Just want to get me a dance with one of them pretty girls. Ain't smelled something sweet since we left Texas."

Nack's face turns sour at the mention of dancing. "I could have won that money easy as pie 'cept for my affliction. You going to see how big your breeches are?"

"I might do some good, if that's what you mean," I say.

Two painted-up women is taking cowboys' money and pinning numbers to their shirts. Rio grins at one of the women, then at me. "Enter the contest, Prometheus Jones."

I look around.

A boy dressed in a plaid prospector's shirt stands with his back to us and spins the cylinder of his gun, slams it shut, and slips it into a fancy holster set loose on his hips. His blonde hair is tangled in greasy curls around the edge of his hat, but something familiar about him sets a cold wash running through my soul.

It's LaRue Dill in the flesh.

CHAPTER TWENTY-ONE

I win a nickname.

"Well, if this ain't just our luck!" Pernie Boyd Dill sits next to his brother and is the first to see me. "Look who showed up, LaRue. Prometheus Jones, right here in Deadwood."

LaRue turns. Omer's whip did good work on LaRue's face. Ain't nothing pretty about it no more; a dark scar runs from his upper lip to the ridge of his nose. There's vengeance in his eyes. "Well, if the devil don't beat all," LaRue says.

"LaRue." I lift my hat and nod. "Pernie Boyd. What brings you all this way?"

"Gold," Pernie Boyd says. "We got a placer stake near Bear Butte Creek not a month ago, and we're set to get as rich as our daddy was before the Yankees stole our money. LaRue done mined a pan of color out of the creek. Better than any folding money around here."

"Color?"

"Gold dust!" Pernie Boyd says. "Gold nuggets. All been found right near our stake. Figure we'd get our bounty out of this gold-rush fever. LaRue says it's our due, being borned gentlemen and all."

Ain't nothing changed about Pernie Boyd. He's as jumpy as a pond frog, talking loud and fast, and saying more than he should.

LaRue frowns. "You here with that cousin of yours?" he asks.

"Here with an outfit from Texas," I say. "Omer done drowned in the Platte coming north."

"Ain't that a shame," LaRue says. His gaze travels over to Rio and back to me. "Any you boys vying for the hundred dollars?"

"Thought I'd give it a try," I say.

"You'll have to win it honest this time."

Rio gives me a glance.

"Weren't no other plan," I say to LaRue. "Just on my way to pay the entry money."

"You might ought to save yourself the trouble," Pernie Boyd says. "I got my rabbit's foot right here, and ain't nobody can outshoot LaRue. He's already killed a dozen Indians. Shot every one of them devils straight between the eyes."

"Didn't know you was such a fine shot," I say.

"Been practicing," LaRue says. He fingers the grip of his Colt. "Self-defense. Never know when you'll have to kill a hostile or a smart-mouthed sharecropper."

"You ever learn to break a horse? Or are you still tricking neighbor-boys into doing it for you?"

Rio steps between me and LaRue and speaks to Pernie Boyd. "So you think your brother will win this little contest, Mr ...?"

"Dill," LaRue says. "Mr. Dill, esquire, to you." LaRue fans his eyes over Rio like he's nothing more than a fresh cow chip.

"Would you care to place a little wager, señor?" Rio asks LaRue.

"You betting on Jones?"

"Sí."

"We don't want your piddly money," Pernie Boyd says. He rolls his rabbit's foot between the palms of his hands. "We aim to win big money on this little venture! Why, I ain't had a day's worth of bad luck since—"

"I'll take his money," LaRue says. "Maybe I can teach him not to get his mouth and his money mixed up."

"Or you may learn to eat your words, no?" Rio puts a finger to the brim of his wide hat, nods, and follows me over to the pay table. "Prometheus Jones, you are my friend, but who are these boys?" A smile hides a worried shadow across Rio's face.

"The sons of the master who owned my mama," I say. "We got some history back home."

"And some trouble, no?"

"We ain't friendly, that's a fact."

"What do they want from you?"

"My hide, I imagine." I ain't anxious to tell Rio the whole story.

Rio drops his smile and looks me straight in the eye. "What do these boys want?"

My anger spills out with the truth. "The Dills said I stole Good Eye out from under them, but I didn't. Won him fair and square in a raffle, but we got in a scrap anyways. LaRue's face got in the way of Omer's whip, and it cut him up, but it was a fair fight. LaRue riled up the crowd against us, so we had to take out and hightail it across the Mississippi."

Rio stares hard at me.

"I ain't no horse thief! Nobody takes a Negro's word against a white man. Not in Tennessee."

"What about Irwin? And your father?"

"I didn't lie. Just left town quicker than I planned."

Rio grins. "So, I will keep a close eye on these brothers, and we can go back to Texas healthy men, agreed?" Rio holds a cigarette between his teeth and lights it with the flame of a match. "But perhaps you can allow them to part with a bit of their gold?"

I ain't letting LaRue get the best of me.

Six cowboys pay their money. The street in front of the livery is full of betting gamblers, prospectors, and a few curious dance-hall girls. Mr. Wheeler is also there, along with Nack, Con, Ole Woman, and Tuttle. I'm number 5. The front man for the contest is the owner of the livery, a man named Roach. He's a slight build with long gray braids on either side of his head. He sports two old Remington revolvers and a cartridge belt over his faded red long johns under a velveteen long-tail coat.

The first event is wild-horse riding, and I win better than easy. Each man is to bridle, saddle, mount, and ride the horse picked for him in the shortest time. My animal ain't nothing but a cussed nag with an evil heart, but I'm in the saddle riding her across the yard in nine minutes. Nothing goes smooth with LaRue's ride, but he ends up in third place. A red-haired cowboy sporting brand-new boots surprises the crowd, winning second in the event. Big Henry comes in last, even with Nack yelling out instructions to him.

Roach lifts his arms to get the crowd hushed. "Everybody having a hog-killing time?" he asks. "We don't have any betting men here, do we?" Roach gins up a set of gold teeth, and one of the prospectors hoots out a cheer.

"Looks like we got us a couple of horse lovers in the competition, but now we're on to the main event. The shooting part of this here contest calls for drawing on a target and then hitting a bull's-eye. Let's see if we got us any sharpshooters in our midst." Roach waves over to a fence at the back of the livery stable.

"For the drawing on a target, each man gets a row of five tins yonder on that gate." Twenty paces from the fence, Roach drags a sturdy stick of green wood across the dirt, while two men set up six sets of cans.

"Now, when I give the amen, these cowboys will draw and unload five chambers on the targets," Roach yells to the crowd. "The last chamber will remain open. The man with the most downed tins wins the round. We'll give you three rounds to prove your stuff."

"Aim low," Rio shouts. I stare down my row of tins and let my hand drift over my holster.

Roach lowers his arms and steps to the sidewalk. "All right, you cowboys, get your irons loaded. Get set. Get ready. Commence firing!"

Gunpowder from six Colts explodes into a storm of noise and smoke. I manage three, but one tin is knocked over on the ledge. One stands untouched on the gate. LaRue downs all five. The other cowboys do some good, but there ain't a steady draw among them.

LaRue spins his pistol back into his belt. "Guess you ain't such a good shot," he says to me.

"Win it now, LaRue!" Pernie Boyd screams.

"Keep your eyes open!" Con yells at Big Henry.

"Reload your pistols," Roach orders.

The second firing is worse for all of us, but LaRue shoots four tins. I put two tins down. The cartridge jams in another cowboy's pistol and it refuses to shoot until he aims just left of his foot. The trigger releases, and the puncher jumps at the sound of the firing, shooting his big toe right through his boot. Blood pumps out into the dirt. The cowboy takes one look and faints dead on the spot.

"Get this city fella over yonder to the saloon," Roach yells out. "He needs a shot of commiseration. Looks like he done got that toe right out of the way."

Two hefty men haul the cowboy out of the lineup.

I load up my Colt again.

"Aim lower, Prometheus Jones!" Rio yells over to me.

"Steady it with your other hand!" Ole Woman cries out behind him.

I drop the loaded pistol in my holster, then practice pulling it through the leather. I hold it fixed with both hands and look down the sight.

"Take your positions, men," Roach yells. "Get set now. Ready. Fire!"

When the smoke clears, I've downed all five tins. LaRue hit four, but he's still three ahead of me.

"That weren't more than luck," La Rue says. "You won't beat me against a bull's-eye target."

"Can't never tell." But I know by the way he handles his iron, there's some truth in his bragging.

A din of angry shouts breaks out between the judges and the red-haired cowboy. "We have a little misunderstanding here, folks," Roach calls to the crowd. "Seems our pardner here loaded up six chambers in his pistol, and as such, he forfeits his standing," Roach shouts over the roar of shuffled bets. "Cowboy numbers 1 and 4 are also done for the day, and we thank you kindly for your efforts," he says.

Big Henry is number 4. The only two left are me and LaRue.

"Now for a grand display of target shooting," Roach says. "Folks, we're down to two men: Mr. LaRue Dill here's a gentleman of the first water from Tennessee, or so he says."

The crowd laughs, but LaRue don't.

"And over here is Prometheus Jones, a genuine colored cowboy from the Diamond Dot outfit in Texas. Time to place your final bets if there's any money not already played out."

A few last prospectors trade small bags of gold dust. I can't judge if the crowd favors LaRue or me.

"For this event, we've got us a bull's-eye target set up. Boys, fetch that wagon!" Two men push an oxcart loaded with hay into the street. A target paper is nailed to its side.

"This is the final round. As such, each man gets one shot. Closest to the bull's-eye wins the round."

"I'll shoot first," La Rue says. He loads his Colt.

"In case you don't shoot best!" someone yells from the crowd.

LaRue shoots it into the air. "You boys might want to be quiet!" he yells. "Don't want to scare me. I might miss my aim, and somebody could get hurt." The clamor of the crowd settles into silence. LaRue turns and takes a long look down the barrel of his pistol. He shoots. Bull's-eye.

"Fine shooting, mister!" Roach says. He looks at me. "Got that in you, boy?"

I take my time loading my Colt. Mama could bring me some luck now if she's a mind. I take up my pistol and aim the sight just below the bull's-eye. The black hole of LaRue's shot is all I can see. LaRue winning this match would be a sin, but I figure God knows that already.

I hold my wrist steady and squeeze light on the trigger. The flash of the shot billows smoke into my eyes.

"He didn't even hit the target," someone yells.

"He didn't even hit the wagon," another man shouts. The crowd laughs, and LaRue smiles up a self-satisfied sneer. "I'll take the hundred dollars from the contest, and another fifty from that fool friend of yours."

Shame fills up my face. I look over at Rio and Ole Woman and see disappointment skirting their eyes. Rio pulls the flask from his boot and holds it up to me in a toast. Fifty dollars lost.

Pernie Boyd collects money from Con and Ole Woman. "No hard feelings, Prometheus Jones," Pernie Boyd says. "You might be good with horseflesh, but when it comes to shooting, you just got outgunned. Too bad your friends lost, too. All they did was give away their money. But I don't mind taking it. Not one little bit."

"You know you're worse than a yelping dog trying to shoot a gun?" Nack throws his money at Pernie Boyd.

"You bet on me?" I ask Nack.

"You ain't nothing but a Jonah, boy," he says. "Bad luck follows you."

Just then, a judge runs up to Roach with the target. They walk over to the wagon and within a minute Roach is waving out to the crowd, shouting at the top of his lungs.

"Holy Joe! Listen to me, men! We got us a regular phenomenon! Beats all I ever seen!" Roach's face is red with excitement. "I ain't a-guessing here ... this is a fact! Upon close perusal of the target, it seems Mr. Dill's shot went dead center in the middle of the bull's-eye." Roach pokes his finger through the hole of the target. “But it seems the second shot, by Mr. Jones, went right into the same hole in the target. Both bullets are lodged in the side of the wagon. The second shot followed the first about perfect. Dang near marvel, it is!”

“What? What about my bet?” someone shouts.

“How’s that possible?”

“Let me inspect that target!” Mr. Wheeler says. “Why, heavens-to-Betsy, he’s right!”

Roach raises his hands and yells out to the crowd. “Since this is such fine shooting and since Mr. Jones here also won first place in the horsemanship and since I done get to declare the winner at my own discretion anyhows, Prometheus Jones is hereby declared Champion of the West and wins the hundred-dollar prize!”

LaRue’s face goes white with rage.

Nack rips the money out of Pernie Boyd’s hand. “I’ll just sort out the winnings now, sonny boy.”

Roach shakes my hand with a steady grip and hands me over a fat pouch filled with gold dust. “That was some elegant shooting if ever there was any! I’d say you’re about the luckiest son of a gun on earth!”

A cheer goes up from the crowd, and Mr. Wheeler pulls me up to stand on the back of the wagon. “Three cheers for this skilled and brave cowboy! Congratulations, Prometheus Jones!” Mr. Wheeler turns to the crowd. “Whatsay we rename him Deadwood in honor of this celebration?”

“Deadwood Jones! Deadwood Jones!”

It ain’t a minute before I’m up on Rio’s and Big Henry’s shoulders being carried down to the saloon, where a room full of men cheer us in the door. “Hip-hip-hooray! Hip-hip-hooray! Hip-hip-hooray!”

Nack comes into the saloon, and for the first time he’s got a smile on his face. “Got our money,” he says. “That kid went running like a whipped dog.” He hands Rio, Tuttle, and Ole Woman their winnings.

Ole Woman grins through his cigar, and Tuttle laughs. “Prometheus done won me twenty dollars,” he says. “I guess it’s time we kept our promise!” Out behind the bar steps a pretty saloon girl with bright red lips, hickory-colored eyes, and warm honey skin.

“Kiss him real good,” Ole Woman says. “He ain’t been kissed since his mama.”

The girl pulls my neckerchief tight to her face and plants a big wet kiss right on my cheek.

Nack fans his winnings before me. “I’m going to get me a wooden foot, and the dang-fanciest boots you ever saw,” he says. “I’ll even let you buy me a whiskey.” He grins at me for the first time since I known him.

“You can buy us all a whiskey, Deadwood Jones!” Rio shoves his winnings into his pocket and orders up a Cutter for the house.

But just as the whole saloon is set to drink to my good fortune, LaRue and Pernie Boyd show up with a tall skinny fellow carrying a shined-up Winchester.

"That's him!" Pernie Boyd yells.

"Prometheus Jones!" LaRue's scar runs deep purple across a wide smirk.

The tall skinny man points the gun square in my face.

"He done stole our horse," LaRue says, "and we tracked him here all the way from Tennessee. He's a lying horse thief if there ever was one!"

The man jerks me out of my chair. "Don't give me no trouble, or I'll shoot you right here," he says. "You're under arrest!"

CHAPTER TWENTY-TWO

I am put on trial.

A storeroom in the back of the outfitter's is my jail. The stink of rotting potatoes fills up the air, along with a hundred or more flies. There's no openings save a small square hole cut in the floor for a man's daily business and a knot-hole carved out from the center of the door for watching the prisoner. The knothole makes for good listening, too, and I put my ear close up to hear Pernie Boyd and LaRue lie to the jailer.

"It's about time this scoundrel was brought to justice," Pernie Boyd says. "He stole a good solid workhorse right from my daddy's barn. Belonged to me. Won it in a raffle, I did. I'm lucky that way." Pernie Boyd's voice is high-pitched and nervous. He knows he's lying.

"I caught him in the act of stealing, and he and his cousin near killed me," LaRue says. "Ain't no Negro boy can cut up a white gentleman and live to tell about it where we're from. You ain't making allowances here, I hope."

The jailer is the owner of the store and saloon, a man named Isaac Brown. He ain't no lawman, just a do-good citizen. "We'll bring this boy to a swift justice. Hold a minor's court in the morning. If he's convicted, we'll have him swinging before sundown."

"*If* he's convicted? You saying I'm deceitful?" LaRue says. I hear the click of his Colt coming out of his belt.

"Now hold on … never said that," Brown says. "Don't need to be so agitated, Mr. Dill. We'll set things right. Just give me till the morning."

I lean back against the thin wood slats of the wall. Is Rio looking for Beck? Beck knows I ain't got it in me to steal a horse, but he don't take to trouble. All I can do is wait and hope the fates is with me.

The foul odor of the storeroom grips my throat. I pull my kerchief over my mouth and nose and slump to the floor, ailing from the heat and the smells. My only good thought is that Omer don't have to be here with me. He and Mama are free of the Dills.

After a while, Brown rattles the keys and opens the door.

"I'll give you five minutes to talk to the prisoner, that's all," Brown says. "And I'll have my rifle on your back the whole time, so don't plan nothing foolish."

"Get out of my way, man," Beck says.

Rio helps me to my feet. "Step out into the fresh air, my friend," he says.

"Glory be, the stench in here is worse than a chicken house. Have you no decent jail, sir?" Beck says. "This lad will as soon smother to death before you get a chance to hang him."

"Where's the marshal?" Ole Woman says.

"Ain't no official lawman in Deadwood," Brown says. "But we got our own way of doing things."

We stand in the open doorway, and I breathe in all the hope that Beck brings.

"I don't know your history, lad, but the brothers won't recant," Beck says. "They say you stole the horse Good Eye from them before leaving Tennessee. I have to ask, is there truth in their story?"

"No, sir," I say. "Won it in a raffle. Ticket give to me by Pernie Boyd Dill for breaking his brother's filly, Miss Stoney."

"Trial's in the morning," Rio says. "The Dills hold a vendetta against you and are pushing for hanging. Your prospects do not look good, Prometheus Jones."

"Ain't no jury going to my side," I say. "I already know that."

"I can't offer much help to you, lad," Beck says. "I don't have the facts firsthand, so it will end up being your word against theirs. I'll speak for your character, but it looks like you made yourself some obstinate enemies. It's a stroke of bad luck you ran on them again here in Deadwood."

Bad luck. "Let them hang me, then. Get it over with," I say.

"Do not give up," Rio says. "*Hasta mañana.*"

"God be with you, lad," Beck says. "Until tomorrow."

That night, I lie awake in the dark. I hate the Dills and every man that ever took up a slave. I hate Omer for letting me talk him into coming west with me. I hate Mr. Jones for not coming to find us. I hate myself for breaking my promise to Mama. I hate everything that can't be undone and made right. Pernie Boyd knows the truth. His rabbit's foot won't save him from God's eternal punishment for lying. I'd like to remind him of that. Then, I laugh out into the night. Maybe I can.

The next morning, the saloon is crowded with prospectors set to witness my ill fortune. LaRue and Pernie Boyd sit in the front row with their righteous faces and black hearts. Beck and Rio sit behind them, with Mr. Wheeler and his notepad, Nack, Ole Woman, Tuttle, and Con. Roach and a handful of cowboys are here for the show.

Brown acts as jailer and judge, with a jury of six men set along one side of the bar. Every juror is white. I'm chained to a chair across from them.

"This trial is now in session, with all firearms checked at the door," Brown says as he downs a shot of whiskey. "Let's get this done. I got a store to run. Prometheus Jones, also called Deadwood Jones, you are accused here of horse thieving by these two fine gentlemen, Mr. Pernie Boyd Dill and Mr. LaRue Dill, from the state of Tennessee in the United States of America. What say ye?"

"I ain't guilty," I say.

"Mr. Pernie Boyd Dill, come up here and tell the court your charges," Brown says.

Pernie Boyd steps forward, clutching his rabbit's foot.

"We ain't got a Bible handy, so I'll do the swearing-in on this here volume of Shakespeare tragedies, which the honorable Mr. Jack Langrishe has lent to this court," Brown says. "Raise your right hand."

"I promise to tell the whole truth, and nothing but the truth," Pernie Boyd says. He sits in a chair in front of the jury. He don't look at me, but his knee springs up and down jittery as a bug the whole time he talks. He stares straight ahead at LaRue.

"Prometheus Jones here stole a good stallion from me that I won in a raffle. Me and my brother tracked him here to bring him to justice. That's what we did. Tracked him right here to Deadwood."

"Tell us the details. What happened?" Brown wants to know.

"The horse was stabled at our home place the night we won her. Prometheus was there to break a filly for my brother, but he took a liking to the stallion. Next morning it was missing, and so was he. Figured he took the horse 'cause it was let out of the stall. We followed him to his uncle's shack, and sure enough he and his cousin had the horse and were set to leave. A skirmish followed, but they got away. We tracked Prometheus all the way here but never found the horse. Rumor around town is the horse foundered, and Prometheus shot it."

"I never shot Good Eye!" I yell. "That horse was as good an animal ever was made by God Hisself. I didn't shoot him, and I didn't steal him neither."

"Order!" Brown shouts. "You'll get your turn to speak, boy!"

I give Pernie Boyd an evil look, and he flinches but sets his eyes right back on LaRue.

"That's all I know about it. But you can see for yourself, he had a hankering for that horseflesh. He always did think he had a special talent with horses, but my daddy said it was just dumb luck. His mama done promoted his high and mighty attitude from the minute he was born. Who would name a colored boy *Prometheus*?"

"Let's proceed," Brown interrupts. "You may take your seat, Mr. Dill."

"Is that all you want me to say?" Pernie Boyd talks straight over to LaRue. "I can say it better now that I've practiced." Pernie Boyd looks over at Mr. Brown. "I'll say it again for you."

Brown don't even look at Pernie Boyd. "The court calls LaRue Dill. You promise to tell the whole truth and nothing but the truth?"

"I always do." LaRue lounges back in his seat and crosses his legs.

"Tell us the events as you know them, Mr. Dill," Brown says.

"Like my brother recited to y'all," he says. "Except the skirmish involved Prometheus's cousin Homer Shine, now deceased. He's the one that cut my lip, but Prometheus is as responsible as if he did it himself. We were bushwhacked. We weren't even carrying weapons of any sort. They ascended on us with an aim of pure wickedness, and it was all we could do to keep them from killing us."

"And you followed Mr. Jones here to Deadwood?" Brown asks.

"We did, sir, for the purpose of bringing him to justice."

"Is that how you've been here a month, my friend?" Rio stands to speak.

"You are out of order!" Brown shouts. "Sit down!"

"We knew he was heading west," LaRue says. "Got a tip from a friendly ferryboat operator." LaRue stares right at me. "Just lucky, I suppose."

"That's all, then," Brown says.

"Not all," LaRue says. "Prometheus Jones is nothing but a sharecropping thief. Any white man believes he's innocent is a fool."

"Thank you, Mr. Dill," Brown says. "Prometheus Jones, you got any witnesses?"

"No, sir."

Beck stands up. "Pardon the interruption, sir, but I'd like to say something on the lad's behalf."

"And you are Mr. ...?"

"Seamus Beck. I run the Diamond Dot outfit. Prometheus Jones has been on my payroll since May, working as a puncher and wrangler. He's been a good hand and an honest lad. His horse did come up lame, and I shot it myself. He's been riding a sorrel of mine since then. Took care of the animal and was honest enough to buy it from me just yesterday. I think these brothers are mistaken."

LaRue jumps up. "You say we're lying?"

"Mistaken, sir," Beck says.

"You got any proof of that?" Brown asks.

"No, sir, I don't. I'm speaking to his character."

"And just what makes your word count? You're just some Negro-loving Irish-dirt immigrant," LaRue says. "You and a bunch of stinking cowboys."

Beck's eyes blaze up, and he pushes toward LaRue, knocking a chair to the floor.

Pernie Boyd jumps up and runs behind LaRue.

"Order! Order!" Brown yells. "Everybody, sit down! Order here!"

Rio grabs Beck and pulls him back to his seat. "Señor Beck, let us not make matters worse!"

Brown turns to me. "You want to tell your side of the story?"

"I never stole nothing. I'm telling the truth. Pernie Boyd Dill gave me a raffle ticket for breaking his brother's filly. I won Good Eye fair and square. LaRue got cut up because he tried to set the mob on me for winning, but all I wanted was to just take my horse and go west. I never stole no horse, so I ain't guilty."

"That all you got to say for yourself?" Browns asks me.

Pernie Boyd about twitches in his chair. He won't look at me. That white boy is afeared to the bone.

"I got one last thing to say." I stand up. My only chance is to get Pernie Boyd petrified scared into telling the truth.

"Proceed," Brown says.

"I feel it heavy on my heart to tell the whole truth and nothing but the truth about Pernie Boyd and LaRue Dill. They're lying about me, for sure, but if I get sentenced to hang, it's my duty to tell what my mama told on her dying bed. Like it or not, we's linked, the Dills and me."

"What are you saying?"

"I was never to speak of it, but my mama was a powerful voodoo sorceress in the quarter. She knew all the spells and black magic of Petro. On the day I was born, she put a great and mighty hex on the Dill brothers so they willn't never mess with me. And nothing can reverse that hex." I look right at Pernie Boyd. "Nothing."

The crowd hums with whispering.

"The hex says the Dill brothers will be in their graves before I will. Now, I know ain't no way in the world of knowing if it's true, but I just feel like I need to tell them boys. If I get sentenced to die, I wouldn't want them to waste a minute of time on this earth 'cause we's all going out together."

Pernie Boyd's face drains to a shade whiter than his shirt. "Take it back, Prometheus!" he yells. "Take back every word of it! Take it back!" Pernie Boyd breathes heavy. "I can't have no hex on me!" He pulls his matted rabbit's foot from his pocket. "I done got me some luck, so you just take that back!"

"Oh, for crying out loud!" LaRue screams at Pernie Boyd. "Could you just act like a man for once?"

"Order! Hush up, all of you!" Brown says as he nods to the jury. "I don't know what foolishness is going on here, but the jury is to disregard any comments from Mr. Jones. Go on into the back room and get us a verdict, men. You heard the testimony. Bartender, sell these onlookers some whiskey while we wait. I don't think they'll be long." The men file out, and I look over at Beck. Anger hangs on his face, but he don't look up. Rio offers me a half smile of pity.

It ain't twenty minutes until the jury is back.

"What say ye?" Brown asks the foreman.

"Guilty!"

"Hanging at noon tomorrow. Court adjourned!" Brown pounds the bar with the butt of his Colt. But it ain't me that gasps out at the news.

Pernie Boyd Dill sucks in a deep wheeze of air and faints dead away.

CHAPTER TWENTY-THREE

News comes from Texas.

"Come on out," Brown says the next morning when he opens the storeroom. "Figure the humane thing to do is feed you before I hang you. Got breakfast coming over."

I squint into the light of the lamp. It's still dark outside. My bones are stiff as an old man's. The chains around my wrists and ankles rub sore on my skin, but it's good to stand and stretch my legs. I breathe deep. "What time is it?"

"You got a few hours before the crowd comes for the show," Brown says. "I made some coffee." He passes a tin of steaming brown water into my hands.

"Much obliged," I say.

"You can sit over there."

I sit on an old barrel next to a window. "What kind of day is it getting to be?" I ask.

"Sunny, if you're lucky. Can't tell yet."

"Good to die on a sunny day?"

"Better than cold and rainy. They'll bury you right away if it's hot and sunny so the buzzards won't get into you."

I set the coffee on the floor and pull out Mama's note from my hatband. It smells of sweat and river water.

Andrew Jackson Jones sold off to
Douglas C. Irwin, Negro speculator,
Lavaca County, Texas, in the year of our Lord 1861

Ain't no use now if my pappy is in Texas waiting for me. I won't lay eyes on him in this world. I tear Mama's note into tiny scraps of paper and let them float out the window, caught up on a gust of breeze.

"You got any family I should notify?" Brown asks.

"Naw. Ain't nobody." Daddy Shine don't need to live my grief.

"They'll bring breakfast over soon. Guess you can sit there until then, but don't try nothing."

I take up my coffee. The morning is a pink shadow over the black hills. One lone star twinkles out of the heavens until it fades like all my dreams about coming west. Nothing turned out. Ain't no talents nor luck nor hope could make me any more than one of Colonel Dill's sharecroppers. It ain't death that kills you. It's life.

I've about finished my breakfast when Rio comes in. "Buenos días, my friend," he says. "Beck and the outfit have gone back to Texas, but I will stay to make arrangements with you and join them later."

"Beck's gone?"

"There was trouble, amigo. The brothers came into the

bar last night. LaRue and Beck traded more words. The boy threatened Beck, then drew on him. Beck grabbed for the gun, and the boy fired into the wall. Beck yanked him up and slapped him. As Beck sat down, LaRue pulled a derringer out of his boot. Nack saw it and shot him. They carried LaRue over to the surgeon. Barkeep called it a fair fight, but Beck didn't think they should linger in town."

"Nack saved Beck's life?"

"Sí. Said it wasn't just for Beck. It was payback for his friend Deadwood Jones."

"His *friend*?"

"Sí. Did you not realize you were his compadre?"

"Letter came in for you last night," Brown hollers out to Rio. He routs around in the mail and finds a small cream-colored square of an envelope.

"From my wife!" Rio smiles. "Perhaps you could read it?"

"I ain't busy."

Rio opens the letter and breathes in the smell of the paper, then hands it to me.

"Perhaps there is news of Irwin."

"It don't matter now," I say, but my hands shake as I take the paper. I read it slow, and my voice trembles to think I might hear news of Mr. Jones.

"To my dear husband,

"I hope to see you soon, Reuel. Our baby comes in October, and the doctor in town says we are well. I

know it is a boy for he kicks hard like a vaquero. The weather is warm, but the breeze off the Frio keeps the heat away from the garden and the house. We are in need of rain. Mother takes good care of me, but I cannot wait for your return. Love to you, my darling. Gretta.

"P.S. I am sorry to tell you that I have learned Mr. Irwin died last spring of the fever and as such, there is no other news of him. G."

Irwin is dead. I hand the paper back to Rio.

"I'm sorry," he says.

"Never counted on no news anyway."

Rio stares at me, then at the paper.

"I guess you got yourself a boy," I say.

Rio nods and starts to fold the letter, but the front door to the outfitter's blows open and Pernie Boyd Dill races in and hollers at Brown.

"Prometheus Jones is innocent!" he yells. "You got to let him loose this minute! I lied. I lied about everything. I admit it standing here. He never stole nothing. Just let him go!"

Rio looks over at me.

"Slow down, son, slow down," Brown says. "We done had the trial. Why you changing your story now?"

"'Cause my brother is dead!"

CHAPTER TWENTY-FOUR

I go home.

"Hold your horses! What happened?" Brown gives Pernie Boyd a worried look.

"You heard what Prometheus said to us yesterday! You were standing there! His mama done put a death charm on LaRue and me. A hex!"

"That's nothing but bosh, boy," Brown says. "Nonsense is all."

"Nonsense, my foot! LaRue died this morning. Shot by one of them fellas from the Diamond Dot. That hex said we'd both be in our graves before Prometheus. I ain't ready to die. I'm too young. You got to let Prometheus Jones go and have him to take that hex off me."

"Your brother was killed?"

"No! Yes! The curse killed him! Can't you see that? It was a fair fight. Happened in front of the whole saloon. LaRue's temper got the best of him, but now he's dead and that hex will be after me! You got to let Prometheus Jones go! My rabbit's foot can't ward off a hex."

Rio breaks in. "He never stole your horse?"

“No! That was LaRue’s idea. He didn’t like Prometheus winning Champion of the West. Said it was an insult. Prometheus never stole nothing.”

“And you lied for your brother?” Rio asks.

“I couldn’t never cross LaRue,” Pernie Boyd says. “He didn’t take to people crossing him, especially blood.” Pernie Boyd falls to his knees. “Please, Mr. Brown, I’m begging you! Let Prometheus out of here!”

“Well, I don’t know what to think,” Brown says. “There’s been a trial. With a jury. We found him guilty.”

“Based on lies!” Rio says. “That isn’t justice! All this boy wants to do is go to Texas and find his father.”

“Find his father?” Pernie Boyd says.

I struggle to stand up in my chains. “You know something about my pappy?”

“You promise to take that hex off me?”

“Tell me!”

“I don’t know that much. …”

“Tell me!” I shout. I’d like to break these chains and grab Pernie Boyd up and shake the devil out of him.

“Your pappy ran away the night you was born.”

“What happened to him?” Rio asks.

“The overseer tracked him down working for the Union soldiers in Nashville, but they said he wasn’t our property anymore. Wouldn’t give him back. Your daddy told he wanted to fight for you-all’s freedom. But didn’t matter one bit what that rascal Lincoln said, the Union boys didn’t want a colored soldiering with them. They put him to work in the kitchen. He died of dysentery."

"But my mama ... She made me promise to go look for him in Texas."

Pernie Boyd shakes his head. "I don't know about that. Must have had her reasons, but don't blame me."

"But why? Why did she ...?"

"Your mama always did talk big about you," Pernie Boyd says. "Like you was better than any of us, white or black. Not that I know anything. I don't know anything at all. Not a thing. But she always did say you was talented and lucky."

"She had dreams for you, perhaps?" Rio says.

"I don't give a diddle-dee-dee about your mammy and pappy," Brown says to me. "I got to figure out what to do. We're going to have to have an inquiry into all this mess."

"No, you're not," I say. I pull Rio's Colt from his belt. "I'm taking a lesson from that Pawnee and breaking myself out of here."

"*¡Excelente,* Prometheus Jones!" Rio takes Brown's rifle from him and pokes it under the jailer's belly. "I need to borrow your keys for a moment, amigo."

"Behind the counter." Brown nods with his hands in the air.

"Lock Mr. Brown there up to the counter," I tell Pernie Boyd. "Once I'm out of town, you won't have to worry about that hex."

"Thank you, Prometheus, thank you. I don't know nothing," Pernie Boyd says. "Not a thing. Nothing. I'm sorry for your trouble. Real sorry." Pernie Boyd backs out the door and runs down the street.

"Your mama really put a hex on that boy?" Brown asks.

"Ain't nothing but words," I say. "Now, where's my gun and my gold?"

"Same place as the keys."

Rio unloads the rifle and locks it in the storeroom. "Don't come looking for us, Señor Brown," he says. "We won't come back to Deadwood."

"Fair enough," Brown says. "Just get going before we get a crowd in town."

"Adiós." Rio tips his hat. "¡Vamos, mi amigo!"

I hand off the Colt to Rio, strap on my iron, and we mount the horses. The sorrel's gait is eager, and we don't linger.

"Where's Beck and the boys?" I ask.

"Waiting for us a mile past camp. Mr. Wheeler offered to help break you out of jail last night."

"He with Beck?"

"As far as Sidney." Rio grins. "He says Deadwood Jones will be a hero in that book he writes. You will be famous, my friend."

We reach the top of the ridge, and I look back at Deadwood. "I guess there's worse things."

Rio motions for us to move on. "You name that horse yet?"

"Thought about it quite a bit," I say. "Leaning toward *Double Dash*."

"*Muy bien.* A fine name for a hero's horse. You must tell Mr. Wheeler." Rio looks over at me. "Are you coming to Texas, then, my friend?"

"Mr. Jones ain't there. ..."

"But perhaps you will be lucky and find a home," Rio says.

The morning sun spins the last clouds into blue, and I smile up at the sky. "I can make my own luck now. Let's go to Texas."

The End

AUTHOR'S NOTE

More than five thousand African American cowboys went up the trail in the heyday of the Texas cattle drives. These cowboys, part of a larger migration of tens of thousands of freed men and women after the Civil War, came west looking for decent wages, just treatment, and genuine independence.

One of these cowboys was a man named Nat Love. Born near Nashville in Davidson County, Tennessee, at the end of the Civil War, Love left his home at the age of fifteen and joined a series of cattle outfits, where he learned to rope and ride and tend steers. With a freewheeling spirit and a Wild West gusto, Love wrote about his adventures in an autobiography published in 1907—the only full-length narrative of an African American cowboy. His affection for the land, his courage, and his confident storytelling paint Love as a man living larger than life in a landscape that is both beautiful and dangerous. Nicknamed Deadwood Dick after winning a roping and shooting contest on July 4, 1876, in Dakota Territory, Love spent twenty years in his "wild and free life" before settling down with a wife and family.

Almost one hundred years after the book's publication—in 2003—I discovered a reprint of Love's autobiography in a University of Nebraska Press catalog and was immediately captivated by his voice, full of adventure and daring, bravado and determination. I was hooked and knew I wanted to somehow write about a boy like Love and his experiences in the West.

Four years and hundreds of research hours later, I have traveled the trails of Kansas and Nebraska, walked the streets of Deadwood, talked to historians and museum curators, read period journals and narratives, pored over old maps and newspapers, and worn out my original copy of Nat Love's autobiography to write a story about a boy's journey west. It isn't Nat Love's story, but it is inspired by his voice, his love of the land, and his sense of adventure.

The historical West wasn't much at all like the West we see on television and in movies. A cowboy's work was dirty and dangerous. It was lonely and boring. Cowboys were young, many in their teens and early twenties, doing a hard day's labor to move cattle across the plains, many times without maps or reliable guides. Food could be plentiful or scarce, but water was always a problem. Cattle and men couldn't survive without water, so each day's journey was planned out to the next river or watering hole.

For the African American cowboy, prejudice and discrimination were present in the form of menial jobs and harder work, but the cattle drive was truly a multicultural place, with black, Hispanic, and Native American cowboys working the range side by side with their white counterparts. Although there were instances of prejudice in the research I read, a man was generally valued for his skill and his work habits. Cowboys received the same pay.

They worked the same hours. They ate around the same campfire. They slept on the same ground. They endured the same hardships.

Some imagine Nat "Deadwood Dick" Love as the inspiration for Edward L. Wheeler's immensely popular character of the same name, the protagonist of a series of thirty-three half-dime adventure novels published for boys during the last quarter of the nineteenth century by Beadle and Adam's. I have taken poetic license and incorporated Wheeler into my story, but there is no evidence that he ever came much farther west than Philadelphia.

While this is an adventure tale of the West, it is by no means a full and complete picture of the complexity of western migration. Cowboys have long captured our imagination, but these men were but a small percentage of the families and farmers and frontiersmen who came seeking opportunity under the banner of Manifest Destiny. Nor does this story give adequate context to the difficulties of Native Americans struggling to survive against this tide of immigration. A more complete account may be obtained by reading nonfiction books and articles about this period in American history.

There are more people to thank on this project than I can possibly attempt within the space of this note. But I would like to acknowledge Kathi Appelt, who read early drafts of the manuscript; Jim Blasingame, associate professor of English education, Arizona State University, who generously offered resources and cowboy poetry; Thomas

Knife Chief at the Pawnee Nation Language Program for his insight; my writers' groups in both Austin, Texas, and Nashville; and my traveling buddies Nancy Chilton and Karen Johnston, who traipsed the back roads of South Dakota and Nebraska with me. Friends indeed.

I would also like to thank my husband, Neil, for his encouragement, and my editor, Stephen Roxburgh. I am truly lucky, both in love and in work.

—H.H.